Duane

Kadance Royal

ROYAL MEDIA
AND PUBLISHING LLC

Royal Media and Publishing
P. O. BOX 4321
Jefferson, IN 47131
502-552-1643
www.royalmediaandpublishing.com
royalmediapublishing@gmail.com

Cover Design: Kamal Designs
Cover Image: Shutterstock Standard License

ISBN-978-1-946111-49-4

Printed in the United States of America

Dedication

I dedicate this book to every Man who wants, needs, actively looking and desperately wants to be loved and give love. ....

Acknowledgements

First, I acknowledge my Lord and Savior Jesus Christ for giving me all of my gifts and especially my gift to write His words.

My husband who is always supportive, loving and encouraging me to utilize all of my gifts and talents. Thank you honey.

To my mother, Dr. Daisy Foree, who is my number one cheerleader and always tells me, "hang in there, you can do it." To my father, Dr. Jack Foree, who is never far away from me in my spirit or heart. I only have to look in the mirror each day to see him.

To Rev. Claude and Mrs. Lillie Royston who support me in everything I do. To the rest of my family, I love you and thank you for your prayers, support and love.

Julia Royston/Kadance Royal

P. S. Why do I write with a pen name? It's about branding and keeping the brands separate. It's another way to create. God created me with many gifts, creative outlets and opportunities and I intend to use them all! Let's go!

Table of Contents

Introduction

Duane has a story just like we all have a story to tell. Duane grew up with little love, affirmation or security. Everything that he loved was eventually taken away. He has a best friend and his mom that love him dearly and are willing to do anything to help him be a man and one day, hopefully, a better man.

Duane knows that he is a hard-working, passionate and fun man but what kind of man is he really? In an attempt to find himself, he finds someone who desperately loves him but how can he give that person the love they deserve when he doesn't know how to love himself? Crossroads. Decisions. Ultimatums. More decisions.

Meet Duane Jackson in Book 2 of the Men of Roberts Junction Series. Enjoy!

Chapter 1

"Run Hank!" Duane yelled.

"No Duane, I'm not leaving you!" Hank exclaimed.

"Yes, you are. You can't fight. You can't take a punch, and I will convince them that it was me and not you,"

"But it was my fault, not yours," Hank said.

"Yeah, but Mama Lori will kill us both if something happens to you," Duane reiterated.

"But I can help," Hank pleaded.

"No, you can't. Here they come. I'll take the blame, but you be there later. Promise?" Duane asked.

"Promise, but Duane I could help you fight," Hank said.

"You can't fight Hank, but you can run so run!"

"Okay, I am going to get help," Hank took off running out of the old boys and girls club to find anybody that could really help.

"No don't get help, just run," Duane closed his eyes, and braced himself while hearing Roscoe and his gang coming down the hall hitting the lockers to scare anybody in their path in that old boys and girls club.

"Duane! Where is my money?"

"I spent it!"

"Spent it on what?" Roscoe yelled.

"Everything I could think of," Duane was sweating and trying to be tough, but he knew that with an inch of his life they could kill him or just break his arm and leg. Roscoe decided on the later because he was in high school and not quite ready to go to "baby jail" as they called it.

Duane lay on his back unable to move his right arm and left leg. Roscoe proved his point to Duane and his boys by breaking one of each and in his words, 'keep Duane balanced.' They all laughed while Duane cried out in agony and waited for help.

Hank came back with Marcus and Deacon in tow just like he promised, but it was too late. It doesn't take long to break a body part when you have four big guys and a sledgehammer.

"Duane! What hurts?"

"Everything fool!"

"I told you I would stay and help you fight," Hank said.

"You can't fight. White boys can't fight," Duane teased.

"Who told you that?"

"I don't know. I just didn't want you to get hurt too,"

"A real stupid best friend you are. Just 'cause I'm white doesn't mean I can't fight. I even rhymed,"

"Oh god, he's a poet and don't know it,"

"Look, Duane, you rhymed too,"

"Shut up and get me to the hospital,"

All they could do was carry him home very carefully. Hank was mad, Duane was crying and Marcus and Deacon were just scared. Duane's parents were angry that they now had a doctor bill and a hospital visit. Once Duane got home, Hank didn't miss a day coming to see him and somehow make it up to him. Hank brought him homework, changed the TV channel or whatever else Duane needed. Hank told him repeatedly that he owed him his life and he would do whatever it took to prove it.

Duane woke up to the sound of the alarm realizing that it was just a dream about his past. He reached over and touched Annette's warm body with her one arm slung across his chest.

"Morning," Annette was always the first to speak as she snuggled closer.

"Morning to you too," Duane said with a low husky voice. Their nights were always filled with hot lovemaking, but Duane didn't like to cuddle or talk sweet talk later. He did allow Annette to touch him while she slept and it seemed to suffice. Duane had his reasons and Annette respected that but didn't like it. She would have loved to be completely wrapped in his arms all night.

"You going in the shower first or after me?" She asked while stretching and sitting up straight in the bed.

"Go ahead. Ladies first," Duane gave Annette a reassuring wink when she looked back at him.

Annette leaned over and kissed him on the shoulder. Duane watched her naked caramel, curvaceous body walk into the bathroom. The shower came on with a hiss and watched the mirror steam. Duane found the remote in the bed and turned on the TV. The breaking news on Channel 5 was 'Robert's Junction is bracing itself for the release of the notorious Roscoe "the rat" James. Formally convicted of racketeering, drug possession with the intent to sell and sentenced to 15 years in prison was released today for good behavior after serving 7 years of his sentence.'

Duane sat straight up in the bed, turned his feet and they slammed on the floor while his heart was beating rapidly. He would have fainted had he not been already sitting.

"Shit," Duane yelled.

"What's the matter?" Annette asked from behind the bathroom door quite concerned at Duane's exclaim.

"Nothing, nothing,"

"Nothing? Something happened on the TV or at work already?"

"No, don't worry yourself about me. I'm fine,"

Annette wrapped a towel around herself, came out of the bathroom and sat next to Duane on the bed. "You sure?"

"I'm very sure. Finish getting dressed before I want to go another round with you and that naked body of yours,"

Annette giggled and blushed all over her light caramel skin, "I have a meeting this morning but I'm all yours tonight. Okay?"

"You better believe it," Duane said with a strange look in his eyes that Annette had never seen before. She had seen him upset before, but this was different. Duane tried to be calm, but fear gripped every ounce of his body despite his calm demeanor.

Duane kissed Annette goodbye at the front door, and he watched her walk down the walk to her car. She pulled out of the driveway and drove to her small office on the river. Duane continued to watch her drive off and whispered to himself, "God keep her safe because I don't know if I can." He got in his Ford Explorer and sped toward the Roberts Junction campus of Indiana University for another day's work.

Chapter 2

Duane pulled into his reserved parking space and greeted all of the guys in the warehouse and loading dock area.

"Good morning!"

"Morning Boss,"

"I don't know about all of that,"

"You got it,"

"With you guys' help, I got it,"

"We got you,"

"Thanks, I appreciate it,"

He had worked with most of these guys for more than 5 years now and even though they called him boss, he still felt like he was one of them. He was the boss and the first one to take the shit was him. Being the #2 man had been great when Hank was the boss, but he was now the boss and must lead.

Duane walked into his office and poured more creamer than coffee into his mug just thinking about how that event 20 years earlier changed his life forever. He remembered so vividly of being on the other side of this desk waiting on instructions from Hank, who now had the luxury of working from home with his wife Jasmine and their twins in carriers nearby.

Duane thought back then that he and Hank would just be teammates on the playground; but after that day, they were brothers for life. Duane always had Hank's back, but he now needed Hank to have his front, back, and life after looking at the morning paper.

Duane unlocked his phone to his favorites and touched the picture of Hank and his whole family's profile picture.

"What's up D," Hank answered on the second ring.

"Nothing much," Duane only had to say those two words to give Hank a hint that something was wrong.

"You don't sound right. Hold on while I get the bottles. Jasmine had a meeting this morning, and I'm all alone," Hank said and Duane could hear the babies in the background crying and cooing while waiting on their bottles. Duane envied Hank just a little with the new babies and wife of his dreams.

"Okay, I'm back. Tell it to me straight. What's up?"

"You remember Roscoe James from school,"

"Yes but I've always wanted to forget. Why are you bringing up that name?"

"They let him out,"

"Like in on the street and out of prison out?"

"One and the same,"

"What are you going to do? You think he's coming for you? What about Annette?"

"I don't know. I hate to admit it, but I am finally scared. Annette is my life, and I don't want anything to happen to her."

"I know exactly how you feel. I was scared too when that crazy girl came after me and Jasmine but I won. I won the jackpot, two beautiful babies and a hot wife that loves me day and night. I'm in heaven. Have you told Annette what's up?"

"No."

"Why not? You have spent your whole life keeping stuff. Trying to be tough. Tell Annette what's up. Stop trying to be tough. It's not good to hide it. Look how much time I wasted not coming correct for Jasmine. Don't do it. Her life could depend on it."

"I know, I know. It's been so long ago why would he want to mess with me?"

"The money."

"They broke my arm and leg for it. I still hurt when it rains."

"True but he's spent a lot of time in jail, thinking, planning and plotting,"

"Don't remind me,"

"Well, tell Annette everything then you plot and plan. Don't sit and wait for him to come for you. Do I need to call Peaches?"

"The cops! Hell, no. Not unless it is absolutely necessary,"

"He's a killer D. You are my brother, and I don't want anything to happen to you. We are supposed to die of old age, not gunshots. I'll follow your lead, and I'll help if necessary but I've got babies and a wife. You should and could have the same. Fix this Duane and don't wait,"

"I know, I know. Thanks, Hank,"

"Welcome. Love you and brothers for life,"

"Peace," Duane said. He never said those three words. The last time he said those words together it had been devastating. He had committed to loving hard in deeds and not just with the words. One day he hoped to get past it, but right now he needed to get through the day.

Duane took a long drink of his coffee and looked through his emails for any additional tasks for the day.

"Duane! Did you see this?" Marcus held out his phone for Duane to see.

"Seen what Marcus?"

"Roscoe is out!"

"Keep your voice down. Let's not announce it to the whole warehouse,"

"Sorry, but I remember that day when he and his boys broke your arm,"

"Don't forget leg,"

"Right, that too. What are you going to do?"

"Why does everybody keep asking me that? I don't know what to do. This is not the OK Corral, and I am not going to call him out like in some western movie."

"True, but you have to do something."

"True, but what?"

"You need protection."

"What is that going to do?"

"Protect! You can't sit here and wait for him to come for you. We need to get the guys from the neighborhood or the cops or something."

"No cops! I can't call the cops then they'll want to know everything. I can't worry about this all day we've got work to do."

"Okay, you are the boss here and of your whole life. So what's first on the agenda?"

"Thanks for your concern. I'm not going to be myself until this over,"

"I understand, but we can help if you let us,"

"I'll think about it and let you know. Let's get to work,"

"Okay, so what's up for the day?"

Duane went through the long laundry list of tasks for the Warehouse personnel to complete all across campus. His work would help to his mind busy from worrying about his job and his sanity. He had the support of his friends and at the present, that's all that mattered.

Chapter 3

"Shock Blocker! Good to see you, man!" Mo Jo was shocked to see Roscoe come through the door. He played it cool because he didn't want to alarm Roscoe by reaching for his gun so he appeared happy to see him instead.

"Good to be seen,"

"When did you get out?"

"This morning. Some reception from you. No car, no food or woman and I've been out 4 hours already. But I heard what you've been up to," Roscoe

"What you mean?"

"Even in the joint, the walls have eyes and ears. You thought you were running things, but I'm home now and about to take over these streets,"

"I'm ready. Whatchu got in mind? 7 years is a long time,"

"True, so first things first," Roscoe took out a gun and shot Morris Bernard Smith, Jr. in the heart. It was his first order of business to take 'Mo Jo' out. 'No!' was the last word that Mo Jo spoke before he took his last breath. Mo Jo's daddy had been

Roscoe's mentor and would have been devastated to know that Roscoe took his boy out. Mo Jo, Jr. had been warned for years by his father to not double-cross Roscoe. Mo Jo, Sr. died at the hands of his mentor, so it was just He took the keys right out of his pocket and said, "Clean that shit up in there," Roscoe ordered to the two guys as on his way out of the old hiding place.

He got in the mint condition Tahoe truck with a fresh wash and started up the engine. MoJo had taken great care of it for the past 7 years. Roscoe looked down and realized it was full of gas, so he floored kicking up rocks in his path. He had walked into the beehive but would be driving out. A steak and a woman was what Roscoe was next on his list. Roscoe thought that his homeboys would have provided that for him automatically. But, nah, them dogs ain't loyal. Roscoe had big plans. Seven years in the big house had given him a lot of time to think. It was now time to put into action the things that had gone on his mind. But, first things first, his body was hungry, and he intended to satisfy it. The other important business would be attended to first thing in the morning.

"How was your day today?" Annette asked while the waiter sat down their appetizer. She touched him on his hand right below his wrist.

"Huh? Did you ask something?" Duane asked surprised and brought back to the present by her touch.

"What is going on are you okay? You have been distant since we got here."

"I'm okay. I've got a lot going on,"

"What's happening on campus?"

"Nothing much,"

"Which is it? A lot going on or nothing much?"

"I just have a lot on my mind! Would you stop asking me that?"

"Sorry," Annette said and took a sip of her wine.

Duane realized that he was wrong and apologized immediately, "I'm sorry. I shouldn't have snapped at you, but I need to work through something and I'll tell you about it later,"

"Okay, I'm just concerned. Can I help?"

"I know that you are concerned and I thank you, but I had rather work it out alone,"

"Okay, but if I can help, don't hesitate to ask,"

"I won't,"

"Well, I have some good news. I have a meeting with a new client on Monday,"

"Great," Duane said still looking out the window of the top floor restaurant.

"Never mind,"

"No, what?"

"You are not listening to me,"

"Yes, I am but I'm distracted and sorry for that,"

"Me too," Annette said regrettably and ate her food in silence.

Duane wished he had the courage to tell her everything, but his dad always said that 'weakness is bad for a man. A man's got to be strong for his woman.' Duane felt like he was strong, but was so full of worry that he wondered if he would be strong enough to bear it all alone.

When they got home, they made love as usual but without the fervor of nights before. Annette turned on her side to face the wall, more worried than ever and thought, 'What is he hiding? Is there someone else? Something is not right.' Duane turned on his side to hide his fear and thought, 'How am I going to keep her safe? I've got to be tough and keep it to myself. I'm the man and she's the woman. She's my woman and I love her, but God help me.' Before Annette drifted off to sleep, she knew what she had to do.

The next day, she called the only person she knew could help her get her questions answered.

"Hello," Jasmine answered on the first ring. She ran outside of the kitchen to the sunroom because the twins had just been put down for a nap, and she was hoping for peace and quiet for at least an hour.

"Boss, how are you?" Annette still called Jasmine boss, even though she hadn't worked for or with Jasmine in 6 months.

"Fine, Annette. What's up with you?"

"Worried."

"Worried? Why?"

"I think Duane is seeing someone else."

"Are you kidding me? What makes you think that?"

"He's distant and standoffish. We make love as usual, but he is preoccupied and not in the moment. I have asked him, but he says he's got a lot on his plate or don't worry about it or he's fine. The more he says it, the more worried I get,"

"Okay, before you or I blow this out of proportion, I know that he loves you,"

"Why doesn't he say it? He has never said he loves me or never actually said the words. He just says, "You know how I feel" and that's it. He shows it, but sometimes a girl actually wants to hear the words said to them over candlelight or face to face while laying on a pillow."

"Remember some guys have a hard time saying the words. Fortunately, Hank is not one of those guys, but Duane is. You do love him right?"

"Right, but I don't want to be played or made a fool of. I am not one of those girls who just ignore stuff and just hopes for the best. If I am the one, let me know. If you want somebody else, let me go. I'll hurt for a while, but let me go."

"The way he looks at you and treats you is what matters. I have seen up close how he looks at you, what he tells Hank about how he feels about you and dreams for you two. There is no question that he wants to be with you."

"Could have fooled me,"

"Well, do you still have a key to his apartment?"

"Yes,"

"Enough said,"

"Point received," Annette said with a smile, and Jasmine giggled in the phone.

Just then Hank opened the sliding door and closed it gently with one hand and the baby monitor in the other. He sat down, placed the monitor on a nearby table and reached for Jasmine's hand.

"Let me ask his buddy and brother. Baby, is something up with Duane?"

"Yes, and I can't tell. Is that Annette on the phone?"

"Yes,"

"Shit! Why didn't you tell me first?"

"Sorry. What's up?"

"I can't tell her. She has to hear it from Duane,"

"He still wants to be with her and everything right?

"Oh Lord, is that what she is thinking? Give me the phone." Hank took the phone from Jasmine. "Annette don't worry about Duane being with someone else. It is far from that. He loves you more than ever. I know that for a fact. He's just got a lot on his plate and on his mind."

"That's what he said. You sound just like him,"

"I know but I promised him, and I keep my promises. Just be patient. I have warned him about keeping this from you, but he is trying to protect you and not hurt you in any way. That's all I can say, but know for a fact that he is NOT seeing someone else."

"Okay, I'll wait,"

"Great. Do you need Jasmine back, because I need a little TLC from her before these babies wake up?"

"No, you can have her. I know you guys only get a few minutes alone, so tell her I said goodbye."

"Will do. Annette says goodbye," Hank said breathlessly, dropped the phone without pressing end and Jasmine giggled. Annette wanted what Jasmine and Hank had. Two kids and they still couldn't keep their hands off each other. Lucky Jasmine. Worried Annette.

Chapter 4

"Miller Enterprises, can I help?" The receptionist asked.

"I need to speak with Mr. Brandon Miller,"

"Who shall I say is calling?"

"Franklin Blocker,"

"Hold on one moment Mr. Blocker while I get him on the line," the receptionist placed the caller on hold and rang Brandon Miller's office, and he picked up the phone on the second ring.

"Yes, Jessica."

"Mr. Miller there is a Franklin Blocker on the line for you."

Brandon fell back in his chair at the mention of that code name for a nemesis that he thought was gone for good. "Put him through."

"Please hold while I connect you with Mr. Miller," the receptionist said to the mysterious caller.

"Hello, Brandon."

"What the hell do you want?" Brandon said quietly.

"Revenge and help from you to get it. You owe me!"

"I don't owe you shit!" Brandon felt his blood pressure going up, his stomach bile rising up past his throat and that sour horrible taste on his tongue.

"Oh yes you do, and I am going to get what you owe me one way or the other. Meet me tonight at the old hangout spot at 9:00 p.m. sharp. Don't be late or the streets is coming to downtown,"

"But,"

The line went dead, and Brandon almost wished he were dead.

Later that night Brandon Miller showed up in a part of town that he had no business. He disguised himself with a jogging suit, hat down low and sunglasses that he bought at a nearby discount store. He felt dirtier than usual from having to change in that filthy gas station bathroom dressed in clothes that he would throw in the garbage as soon as he got home. He wanted no one to recognize him or even try to associate him with his rich world.

"Miller why you dressed like that?" Shocker asked.

"You know why? Why in the hell am I here?"

"You owe me. I went away for 7 years for you. It's going to cost you. Big time,"

"How much?"

"Seven million."

"You must be out of your damn mind!"

"No, I found my mind and found it in jail for 7 years. You owe me a million for each year I was in that hole, eating nasty food and fighting bastards every day."

"You can't prove shit."

"Want to bet?"

"The only person there was me, you and Stone."

"You sure?"

"Sure I'm sure. You killed Stone, and that was why you went to jail for it."

"Well, you seemed to have forgotten that Stone was trying to kill you, and you were not packing. I saved your life that day. Probably don't have a piece on you now."

"Nope!"

"Dumb bastard. Why would you come to the West End without backup? Do you not listen to the news or know what part of town you in? Stupid."

"I might be, but I wasn't dumb enough to go to jail for 7 years. So you gonna kill me now?"

"Not before I get my money, and then we will see if you live or not."

"So what's the deal?"

"The deal is you will meet here tomorrow with $50,000 in a black suitcase. Next, you will wire the rest of the money to this account."

"Look at you. Big time with the off-shore accounts."

"I'm not as dumb as I look."

"Apparently."

"What do I get?"

"For this video not to be on the news,"

"What video?"

"This one."

Shocker pushed the button and the video began to play.

"How in the hell you get that locked up for 7 years?"

"I have my ways."

"Shit!"

"Right, see you tomorrow."

Brandon walked speedily out of that abandoned warehouse knowing that he had to head to the bank the first thing in the morning. Once safely in his car and on the road, he made one call first.

"Yeah," the voice said on the line after only 1 ring.

"I need a favor."

"What kind of favor?"

"The killing kind."

"My favorite kind."

The line went dead, and Brandon smiled all of the way to his mansion.

Annette woke up the next day stressed and excited all at the same time. She had a meeting with a potential new client that she knew could take her business to the next level. She knew that once she had a contract with the client, hopefully, she would be able to concentrate on Duane and discover what the problem was that was keeping his attention away from her. Today, she had to focus on impressing this client to get their business. She dressed in a cute suit with a knee length skirt, medium heels and a bag to match. She was a geek at heart, but she knew how to dress professionally when necessary.

"Where are you going today?" Duane said as he stood in the bathroom doorway and saw her already dressed.

"You forgot or didn't listen."

"Okay, you have a meeting today with some client."

"You were listening."

"I'm always listening to you, even if I don't act like it." Duane lied.

"That's good to know. I thought I was talking to myself," Annette smiled, and Duane knew that he had covered his tracks really well.

"Never baby." Duane almost said he loved her, but caught himself just in time. He also had forgotten about her meeting but knew that she only wore that suit to meet a new client. He was proud of Annette and her accomplishments. He knew it was wrong not telling Annette exactly how he felt, but he hoped to one day do what Hank suggested and say the words.

"How do I look?"

"Good enough for me to want to take it off of you."

"Nice to know."

"What time will you be home?"

"It's a lunch meeting, so I should be home on time."

"Great. Maybe we will go out and celebrate tonight?"

"Sounds good to me. Thanks for the coffee. I needed it because somebody kept somebody up a little late last night."

"You are welcome, and I think that somebody was me. You regret it?"

"Never," Annette said as she grabbed her purse off of the bed and headed to the bathroom doorway.

"That's good to know."

"Well, I am headed out."

"Goodbye."

"See you later. I don't like goodbye."

"Okay, see you later."

"I love you."

"Peace."

Annette turned her head up and received Duane's kiss before she walked out the door. She thought, 'Peace? Who the hell says peace to their lady?' She shook her head and remembered what Hank said. She would be patient, but she didn't know for how long. She raised the garage and backed her car onto the street. She noticed that Duane's truck was still parked outside of the garage. She guessed he hadn't felt like driving it in.

Duane shook his bowed down head and was upset with himself that he didn't or couldn't seem to say I love you back to Annette. He remembered the last time he told someone that he loved them, and he promised himself that he would never do it again. He finished getting dressed, opened the front door, pushed the button to unlock his door and his truck exploded. His truck's debris went all over the yard. He dodged any debris from hitting him by closing the front door quickly. People came running from their other condos as they saw the flames go high into the air. Duane slowly opened the door and watched his SUV burn up. He knew who and why. He called the only number he knew.

"Hey D, what's up?"

"He just blew up my truck."

"What! I'm on my way."

"NO! Stay home, I don't want you near me."

"I'm coming D, and you can't stop me. Jasmine is home today, and I'm on my way."

"Hank!" Duane yelled into the phone but heard the line go dead.

"Babe, I've got to see about Duane. I'll be home soon."

"Take care sweetie and be careful. I know that something is up and whatever it is, just come home to me and the babies."

"I will," Hank gave her a hard kiss that excited but scared Jasmine all at the same. She knew that something was going on with Duane, but she knew that she couldn't alarm Annette. Hank didn't tell her what was going on, and she didn't ask. She kept feeding the babies the formula and said a prayer.

Hank pulled up moments later to fire trucks, the police, Duane's insurance agent and an upset Duane.

"Sir, you can't go any further," the firemen said as Hank got out of his truck and was moving closer to Duane and the burned up truck.

"It's okay! Let him through, let him through," Duane yelled.

Hank walked closer to Duane and saw the look in his eyes that he had seen so long ago after Roscoe and his goons broke his arm and leg. It was fear. Cold fear.

"D, man this is terrible,"

"I know. It was a warning,"

"Even worse. The cops are asking questions."

"How did you get your car out of the garage?"

"I drove to get the coffee for Annette and never used my remote until I walked out of the house to leave for work. The truck was unlocked in the garage. When I went to the coffee shop, I didn't lock my door because I could see it from the counter. I didn't lock it back with the remote when I got back home because I knew I was leaving shortly and people know my truck in this neighborhood. Whatever damn device that they used must have activated on the remote only."

"This sounds like something out of a spy movie, and shouldn't be happening to one of my closest friends who works hard every day and in love."

"Right. What am I going to do now?"

"You've got to tell Annette for sure now. You can't wait another minute. They know where you live, so you've got to come and stay with me in the country. You can't come back here. Get your stuff, and we'll get stuff for Annette later."

"I'm not putting you, Jasmine, the babies, and Annette at risk. Listen, can I stay at Mama Lori's old house until this is over. I'll bring Annette to your house, and she can stay with you guys."

"Yeah, but it hasn't been lived in for 6 months. I just need to turn on the electricity."

"I don't care about that, just call and I'll pay you back,"

"Don't worry about that. We've got to get this problem solved and quickly. What about work?"

"Marcus has got that on lock for me today. This is Friday, so we should be good for now."

"Where is Annette?"

"She has gone to work and had a big meeting today with a new client. I want her to do well today, so I can't tell her until she gets off work. I will meet her and tell her tonight."

"D, don't chicken out. You've got to protect her. They blew up your truck. They'll kill you and her for what they want. I know you don't want to hear this, but we have to call Peaches."

"You are right. I don't want to, but I have no choice now."

Duane went back in the house gathered some things in a bag, stayed until the fire department cleaned up everything and the police took his truck away for inspection. It was now a police matter and an investigation into the cause of the explosion. Duane got in Hank's truck, and they headed to the police station to talk things over with Officer Pamela Simpson; better known as Peaches.

"Chief, you should have seen it. The truck blew up and everything. The hood shot up in the air like a missile."

"That's good. I would have loved to have seen his face when his truck blew up."

"He was scared shitless. I told you my blow up guy was good. It was perfect. Why didn't you want him dead?"

"It's an old score. I can't kill him 'cause of the code."

"Right. By the way Chief, Duane's got a girl. We followed her to work. It looks like she's some tech geek with her own company."

"That's good. Keep an eye on her. It could prove handy. Let me know her every move today. Good work,"

"Gotcha. We out."

Chapter 5

"This is Annette Wilson of AJ Technologies, how can I help you?"

"Ms. Jackson, this is Mr. Miller's secretary. He is unable to meet you for lunch at 12 but would like to meet you for an early dinner at 4:00 p.m. Are you available?"

"Yes, I am. Where shall I meet him?"

"Ruth Chris East. Do you need that address?"

"No, I know its location."

"Thank you and have a great day."

"You as well," Annette hung up the phone disgusted that she would be late getting home and meeting Duane this evening. She would be sure and make it up to him later, but her focus had to be on this meeting because her business depended on it.

She texted Duane and told him that she would be late, but would see him later tonight.

He texted back, 'fine.'

She texted back, 'I love you.'

He texted back, 'peace.'

'Who does that?' Annette thought, but she knew the answer immediately. Duane does that. Annette took the rest of the day preparing for her meeting at 4:00 p.m. She had been working on some new security and tracking devices. She hoped to test them out soon to get them to the security market. Human trafficking is at an all-time high, the tech world was trying to help. The demand was there for new tracking devices without the insertion of the chip in the body which was more and more popular. Her potential new client was very interested in her new discovery and wanted to invest millions to get this through research quickly and on the market.

Meanwhile, Hank and Duane met Peaches for lunch.

"So what have you two gotten yourselves into this time? I have never seen two people who start out as janitors, then building operators and now big time corporate people get themselves in so much trouble. Tell me the truth."

"Peaches, it started back in the day with Roscoe. You know his daddy dated my mama. Some people say his daddy was my daddy, but my mama said no.

He has hated me and had it for me ever since. I don't know why, because he did nothing but torment me all of the time. His dad was big in starting the local gang, and he was sure to turn it over to Roscoe. He wanted me to join the gang, but my mama said no. He was big and mean, but my mama stood up to him and said no. I spent a lot of time at Hank's house and with you guys because of it. I found some money that Roscoe stuffed in my mattress at the house and wouldn't return it. He and his friends broke my arm and leg because of it. My mom let me stay at Mama Lori's house and that is the long and short of it. I told him that I spent the money, but I didn't it. I have double and tripled that money over the years. I've always lived low key and plan to keep it that way. I don't know what he went to jail for, but I assumed it was murder, drugs or both. Why he is after me is beyond me? He could have killed me long along, but he didn't. So why is he coming for me now?"

"Revenge. Jail gives you a lot of time to think. He made a list of everybody he hated. And even though you thought he forgot, he didn't. I can find out why he went to jail, and who he was linked to when he went to jail. My problem is you staying safe until we have reason to arrest him or something else goes down."

"He wants to stay at Mama's house, but I don't know if that is safe because it is right in the middle of the neighborhood."

"I don't suggest that. You got somewhere else to stay?"

"He can stay with me," Hank said.

"Nope, not with them baby cousins of mine there. How about the cabin in Mayorsville?" Peaches asked.

"It's been closed up for a few months, but it should still be good. Nothing out there but the deer," Hank said.

"Thanks, no phone access or no TV. Wait until I tell Annette about that."

"She'll hate it, but she'll be thankful after this is over. By the way, where is Annette?"

"She is meeting some new client."

"Do you know who it is?"

"No! I think she was going to tell me, but I've been too preoccupied with this Roscoe thing."

"You should ask her who she is meeting, and just act like you are wishing her luck and not make her suspicious,"

"Really? I don't usually do that. It might make her trip out,"

"Maybe, but you should know. Roscoe is tricky. He may try something. If he hit you at your house, he knows or one of his soldiers know that she is there. Remember they like to hit where you hurt most. He hit your car first. He could come for your woman second. Text her and ask her."

"I guess it couldn't hurt."

"Man, you are a mess. Do it!" Hank said.

Duane dialed the number and waited for her to answer. She answered on the second ring. "Hey, Duane. How are you?"

"Fine. Well, I was thinking about you and kind of wanted to wish you good luck today with the new client. Can you tell me who you are meeting, so I can keep my fingers crossed?"

"This is unusual. You've never asked before? You jealous?"

"Well, that's it. I'm jealous."

"Well, that's nice to hear. I'm meeting Brandon Miller of Miller Enterprises. He is a billionaire horseman that also dabbles in construction, and wants to know more about my tracking devices to hopefully invest in them and help get them on the market."

"Sounds nice. What time are you meeting him?"

"For an early dinner at 4:00 p.m."

"Where?"

"Ruth Chris East."

"Wow, you said he was rich so I guess that is a normal place that rich folks would want to eat."

"You must be rich too because you took me there for my birthday remember?"

"Yes, I remember. Well, it is almost 2:30 now. What time are you leaving out?"

"In about an hour."

"Well, be safe and I'll see you later,"

"Will do. Love you."

"Peace out."

Duane hung up the phone and was about to relay the answer when Peaches interrupted. "Who says 'peace out' to their girlfriend?"

"He does with his dumb ass. I told him to tell her that he loves her, but he won't,"

"I have my reasons, and she knows I love her."

"No, she doesn't. Screwing her doesn't mean you love her."

"I'm faithful. I'm loyal. I please her, and she has a key to my condo."

"You are a dog with a condo," Peaches said and Hank laughed.

"A dog with a condo, what kind of shit is that?" Duane asked.

"True shit. Dogs are faithful, loyal and please mankind. They just don't own condos."

"Get out of here Peaches," Duane said.

"I will. Tell me who she is meeting."

"His name is Brandon Miller. I haven't heard of him."

"He's a billionaire horseman who is spreading his wings and making big moves in the city. He has some underground connections. He's not clean I can feel it, but the rich white man never goes to jail. My brothers do. No offense Hank."

"None taken. I've been in and around the family too long to be offended. I wish I could change it, but I can't. You know I know," Hank said.

"Something is up, and I don't know what but it should surface soon. I've got to get back to the station. You guys have kept me long enough. Thanks for lunch, and I'll let you know if I find out anything. Bye, you two and be safe."

"We will Peaches. Love you and thank you," Hank said.

"Love you both," Peaches said as she exited the restaurant.

"Thanks, Peaches," Duane added.

Duane and Hank headed down to Duane's insurance agent to pick up a check to get a rental car for 5 days until the police could get everything sorted out with his burnt up car. With a rented car, Duane hoped that he could be disguised from Roscoe and his soldiers.

Annette arrived at Ruth Chris and handed the valet her keys. She was 10 minutes early, so she would have an opportunity to visit the ladies room one last time to check out her face. After taking care of business, she came out of the restroom to see a very handsome man standing at the hostess station notifying the young lady that a guest would be joining him.

"Mr. Miller," Annette interrupted him.

"Yes,"

"I'm Annette Joh-,"

"Yes, you are. Excuse me, but you are even more gorgeous in person," Brandon interrupted her from finishing her last name.

Annette blushed slightly behind her light caramel skin. Brandon could see that she enjoyed his compliment despite her calm demeanor. "Thank you. It is a pleasure to meet you," Annette said as she extended her hand.

Brandon shook her hand but held on to it just a little too long for her comfort. He also placed his other hand on top of hers and rubbed it slightly.

Clearly, a double meaning was conveyed. "The pleasure is all mine. Shall we? After you."

Annette headed to the table following the hostess. The hostess was about to pull out her chair, but Brandon stopped her, "Allow me." He leaned in to smell her perfume before standing to be seated.

"You smell divine."

"Thank you," Annette knew right then that she was uncomfortable and must quickly turn the attention to her presentation. She put her small briefcase on the table and opened it to get out her notes.

"Let's eat first and not talk business right away."

"Alright," Annette said as she put her papers away.

"Have you lived in Louisville all of your life?"

"Yes, I was born in the South end of town."

"Wow, I was born in the Lexington area in the heart of horse country. I loved horses, and knew that one day I would work hard enough to be able to afford one or a slew of horses,"

Unbeknownst to both of them, there were two men sitting at a small bar that was in a secluded area, but the view was to the entire dining room.

"Chief, he's going to be late because he is at Ruth Chris with a gorgeous babe right now,"

"The Hell he will be late, Butch. I'm going to call him and get his ass out of there."

"They just got the salads," Butch said.

"Let him eat it. That will be his last meal," Chief said.

"Wait a minute. Ain't that the girl we saw this morning?" Mouse asked.

"Yes, it is," Butch said.

"What did Mouse say?" Chief said.

"I think the babe with Miller is the same chick we saw leaving Duane's place."

"Have I hit the jackpot? I'm one lucky bastard. I can literally kill two birds with one stone. I can't kill Duane, but I can kill what he loves. Bring them both to me."

The server took away the salad plates. "Can I show you my designs now?"

"Honestly I don't care what you design. I'm buying it and investing in it. As soon as I saw you, I knew I wanted whatever you had. I mean whatever your company's services provide, I want to invest in," Brandon said as he leaned across the table toward her.

Annette was immediately uncomfortable, flattered and aroused all at the same time. She scolded herself for being the slightest bit attracted to this man. She couldn't be attracted to this man because she had only met him 10 minutes earlier. Sure she did a Google search on him and he was attractive, but she loved Duane. In that instance she knew that it was the things that he said, the way he said it and not just how he looked. It was sexual to say the least because his eyes roamed her body while he spoke the words. She had been with Duane a year and hadn't heard him say those words in that particular way as this man had. She knew that she would have to be extremely careful around him in any future business dealings.

The steaks arrived and fresh bread, but Brandon's phone rang just as the plates were set on the table.

"Miller, are you standing me up?"

"No, I'm in a meeting."

"You have an hour to get to me. That means 30 minutes to finish whatever you are doing, and then 30 minutes to bring me my money,"

"Fine."

"I got yo fine, and I will have your ass if you are not there in 1 hour."

Butch's phone rang again and he knew who it was, "Pick them up and bring them to me after they pay for the check,"

"Will do Chief,"

Chapter 6

Butch and Mouse headed for the door and waited for Brandon Miller and Annette to leave the restaurant. It was only a short time later that they both exited the building. Annette thought she was headed to her car, but Brandon stopped her.

"Annette, do you have somewhere to be? I have something that I need to show you at my office. Would you ride with me somewhere?" Brandon asked with a smile.

"Well," Annette hesitated, because she was torn between making this meeting as productive as possible and hopefully, signing a contract in her portfolio and meeting Duane. She knew that this deal had the potential to change her life and her business forever, but she was excited about seeing Duane and telling him everything that happened whether he heard her or not.

"It won't take long I promise. I just forgot to bring some things with me that are in my office," Brandon pleaded with that smile that he knew was hard to resist.

"Okay, but let me call my boyfriend first and let him know that I'll be late," Annette said. Annette dialed

Duane's number, but he didn't answer. She left a message explaining the situation and that she should be to him by 8. Annette turned and followed Brandon to his car. Once he settled her in her seat, he walked around to the driver's side to be seated. When he opened his door, Mouse opened Annette's door, threw her purse and briefcase on the ground and forced his way into the car.

"Drive Miller to where I tell you. My boss is waiting. Don't make a move or she gets it. I'm not playing," Mouse said as he showed Brandon the gun at Annette's side. Annette could feel the gun in her right rib cage. Her mouth went dry, and she began to panic. She knew that she had to keep her wits about her because her very life depended on it. She had been in this type of situation when her old boss Jasmine had been a target of someone wanting to kill her. This was totally different. As much as she wanted to cry and scream, the look on Mouse's face knew that she should keep quiet and just think. He could open the door and just throw her out anywhere. She had read recently about the security risk of technology inventors, and as much as she didn't think she was a risk in the Southern Indiana Kentucky area she now knew better.

"Shit man, I was going to meet him. He didn't have to go to this extreme!" Brandon said nervously, as he was trying to keep the car under control.

"You sit in jail 7 years, and you see how patient you are. Just drive," Mouse ordered.

Annette could see the direction that they were headed and knew that they were going to a downtown area. She wished she had gotten Duane on the phone to tell him what was going on, but there was no use. She made no sudden moves and held on tightly to her purse and briefcase.

Annette was in the middle of the front seat and could see that they were being followed by a black SUV. She was going to try out her new inventions. She touched her nose ring, her earrings and bracelets.

Meanwhile, Duane and Hank were still at the rental car company getting everything situated for Duane's rental. They were about to leave when Duane felt his phone buzz indicating he had a message.

'I'll get that later,' Duane thought when he saw the message was from Annette.

"You okay guy? I've been out long enough and have to get home to Jasmine and the babies. Call me if you need anything," Hank said as he walked to his truck.

"I'm good. I just got to get this car and then meet Annette. She just sent me a message that I will check in a moment,"

"I'm out. Keep your head up, and I love you,"

"Peace," was all that Duane could say. Hank just shook his head and thought, 'Duane is never gonna change.'

When Hank got in his car, he called home. "Hey, babe."

"Hey, everything okay?"

"Yeah finally. I'll explain everything when I get home. You need me to bring anything home for you guys?"

"Nope, just you,"

"Girl, that's what I like to hear."

"You better believe it. Let's put the babies down early and see what trouble we can get in,"

"I'll meet you in the shower,"

"Definitely."

"See you in a few."

"Okay, love you."

"Love you more."

Hank hung up the phone with a smile thinking just how blessed he was. He wanted so much for Duane to have what he had, but that was Duane's decision not his. In the meantime, he pushed on the gas to get home faster to Jasmine and his babies to hold and kiss them good night.

When Duane sat down in his rental truck, his phone rang and the caller ID said, 'Xavier.' He remembered Annette saying, that if he ever got a call from someone named Xavier that it wasn't good.

"Hello Xavier, what's up?"

"She's in trouble."

"Who's in trouble?"

"Annette's in trouble. Somebody's got her, and she is trying to tell me who and where."

"How do you know that?"

"Her inventions. I know she's told you about them."

"Yeah, but I wasn't paying attention."

"Well, I hope you are paying attention right now bruh because her life depends on it. According to her message, someone has kidnapped her and taking her somewhere along with the Brandon client. They keep calling the boss' name 'Chief' and the guy in the car is named Mouse. Do you know them?"

"Nope, but I'm about to find out."

"I'll keep an update on where she is. But I need to call the police or something, so they can rescue her or something."

"Just keep tabs on her. I'm calling the police."

"Okay, let me know something soon. They are headed into the West End of town near the warehouse district."

"Good to know. Keep your phone handy. I'm going to be calling you back very soon,"

"I'll wait to hear from you, but hurry,"

"I will. Thanks, Xavier. Peace,"

Duane's mouth is dry, and he realizes that he may never be able to tell Annette anything again if he doesn't find her fast.

He dials his lifeline, "Hank! Oh my God man, somebody's got Annette!"

"Calm down, who has Annette?"

"I don't know, but Xavier said."

"Who is Xavier?"

"Annette's assistant. He said that she is using her new inventions, something I didn't pay attention to, to get messages to him that she's in trouble. Oh man, I have been so stupid. I should have done and said so many things. Why, why, why? This is crazy! I love Annette and have for the past four years. What have I been waiting on?"

"Yes, you have been stupid, stubborn and hard headed, but we can't worry about that now. We really need Peaches. Hold on, and I will patch her in on 3-way,"

"Officer Simpson speaking, how can I help you?"

"Peaches help! Somebody's got Annette!"

"Who? Calm down Duane. Talk to me."

"Xavier is Annette's assistant, and she has invented some new stuff to track down people. She was doing a demonstration today like I told you, and she met him at Ruth Chris in the East End. She is now using that stuff or jewelry or whatever on her body to tell Xavier that she's in trouble and headed to the warehouse district in the West End."

"Okay, is she still with Brandon Miller?"

"Yes, that's what she said."

"I did some digging, and he was somehow connected to Roscoe during the investigation that sent him to prison. As usual, Miller got off and Roscoe went to jail for 7 years. Roscoe got out, and he could be getting revenge."

"Can you patch in Xavier to me too?"

"I'll try. I am so nervous I can't think straight. If anything happens to Annette, I swear I will."

"You will do nothing while an officer is on the phone. It can be used as evidence.

"Shut up Duane and get the assistant on the phone," Hank warned.

"Thanks Hank for getting him before I had to go off," Peaches said.

"Well, can you blame me?"

"No, but dial the number fool!" Peaches added.

"Okay,"

"Xavier, here. What did you find out?"

"Nothing yet, but I have Peaches Simpson a police officer on the phone and Hank. What can you tell us?" Duane asked.

Xavier began to relay all of the information that he had already told to Duane.

"Is there a camera on any of her devices or is she just using the code?" Peaches asked.

"There is a camera on her nose ring and she is videotaping everything that is going on now."

"Perfect. Is there a way to patch in and see the video from where you have there?"

"Yes, but we would have to have permission to tap into your system,"

"I'll ask. Keep tabs on her now, and let me get with my superiors. Duane, you sit tight and don't do anything,"

"Peaches! I've got to do something?"

"Duane, don't do anything!" Peaches yelled.

"Listen to her Duane. We need you and Annette safe instead of you both ending up dead. I lost the only mother I've ever known. I'm not losing my brother,"

"Calm down both of you. I feel the love, but we have to keep our heads about us. Xavier are you still on the phone?"

"Yes, ma'am."

"I'm going to send you a text, so I will have your phone number. I can see all of your numbers on my phone, so I can call you back. Duane don't do anything until you hear from me. Hopefully, we'll be calling you to come pick up Annette safe and sound. You hear me? Hank, go home to your wife and babies. "

"Okay," Duane said sadly.

"Almost home now," Hank said.

"I'm still old enough and strong enough to give you a good whooping," Peaches said sternly.

"I know. Thanks, Peaches," Duane said.

"Thanks, Peaches. I love you," Hank said.

"Love you too both."

"Call me later Duane," Hank said and hung up.

"Xavier stay close to the phone, and let's get Annette back home safe and sound,"

"I'm ready," Xavier said. Xavier and Peaches began working on connecting their networks to follow the movement of Annette, Brandon Miller and the two goons leading them to the hideout. There was only a matter of minutes before they could possibly lose the connection, and the ability to see what was going on through Annette's technological jewelry.

Hank pulled the car in the garage shortly after the phone call. He walked into the kitchen to find the two babies on the table in the baby seats, and Jasmine feeding them one spoonful at a time. She had two bowls, two spoons and two beautiful babies. Hank stood and watched for only a second at the two little ones calm, kicking their feet, flinging their arms and happy as each spoonful of dinner went into their mouths, and they saw their dad. Hank was overcome with emotion.

"Hey babe," Jasmine said not immediately turning around.

"Hey," Hank finally said.

Jasmine realizes that it took a minute for Hank to say anything or come closer to her in the kitchen, so she turned and saw the tears streaming down his face. She stopped immediately, "What's the matter babe?"

"I can't lose this,"

"Lose this? Lose what?"

"Lose you all. I just can't,"

"Oh babe, we are not going anywhere. I love you. The babies love their daddy. Come here. What happened?"

"Nothing. I'll tell you later. Let's get the babies down, and then I'll tell you. I love you. Always remember that," Hank said as he walked over to Hank, Jr., picked him up out of the baby seat and carried him to continue feeding him.

"I love you too, but you are scaring me,"

"It's going to be fine. I just need a spoon," Hank carried Hank, Jr. to the living room and held him close as the baby ate. It didn't matter if the peas went everywhere including his shirt. Hank just needed to hold something that he loved and not let it go.

Duane was pacing back and forth like an animal in a cage. He didn't know if he would ever see Annette again. He knew that he had made so many mistakes, but prayed to himself that if given another chance he would do better. How would he ever explain to her all that was in his heart? How would he make it up to her and give her the love from his heart, and let the words come out of his mouth and just not the actions shown with his body? How did he not notice the alarms on his phone? Why hadn't he called her back earlier? Even if she didn't answer, he could have called. The perfect sight was always hinder sight, but what did that matter now? Annette was kidnaped. It wasn't a movie. It wasn't in another town or country, it was in the Louisville Southern Indiana area in the heart of the Midwest. He remembered all of the times she said, "You know I love you right?"

He would just say, "Yeah, thanks." Who in their right mind doesn't say I love you too? She deserved that. He deserved that. He might have just messed up the best thing that ever happened in his adult life.

Her face would always be begging for an answer even if she didn't ask him to say the words or actually beg for the words to be spoken. Her eyes were speaking volumes, and he still resisted.

Looking at her desk, Duane noticed that the computer was unplugged. "Shit, why is this unplugged? She told me never to unplug this!" He quickly plugged in the computer and it came to life. He quickly typed in the password which was luckily something he would never forget, his middle name, "Harvey." He hated that name and wished his mother had named him something else, but that was unimportant right now. Getting Annette back must be his top priority. He looked at the screen and realized what he was seeing. Duane grabbed his keys and headed for the door.

Once in the car, he dialed his lifeline. "Hank!" Duane yelled into the phone.

"What D?" Hank said groggily and sat up quickly on the bed. He tried not to awaken Jasmine, but it was too late. As a mother, she was more of a light sleeper than ever.

"Babe, what's going on?" Jasmine asked.

"It's D," Hank put his hand over the mouthpiece to answer her.

"Oh Lord," Jasmine said.

"Roscoe's got Annette!"

"What? Roscoe! How did he get Annette?"

"It's a long story, but can you call Peaches?"

"Yep, calling now. Hold on." Hank pressed the few buttons to conference Peaches onto the phone.

"Hello, Hank?" Peaches asked.

"Peaches, Duane's on the other line. Go D,"

"Peaches! Roscoe's got Annette,"

"We know Duane! Do you ever answer your phone?"

"I'm sorry. I was waiting on Annette's call and got distracted,"

"Boy, thankfully her assistant Xavier stayed with us and the police are on their way and should be where her signal is leading us now,"

"It's the old hideout, isn't it? I recognized the sign on the wall, 'family for life' right?"

"Yep, you got it"

"I'm on my way too."

"D, do you need anything from me?"

"No!" Peaches and Duane answered simultaneously.

"Stay at home with your wife and them beautiful babies, the police have got this,"

"Hank, I would die if anything happened to you, and then Jasmine would kill me again," Duane insisted.

"Alright I'll wait here, happily and nervous but D, call me when this is over. Love you both and thanks, Peaches,"

"Welcome, love you too. Get there Duane!"

"I'm on my way! Bye!"

Meanwhile across town, "Chief we're here," Mouse said on his phone. He had Annette by the arm, and she was tapping even harder on her bracelet. This was her only connection to the outside world of this hell she had been snatched into. She didn't know who she was angrier at Duane, Brandon or herself. She was innocent in this whole maze. She was just trying to close a business deal. Now, it looked like she would be a body found in a warehouse on the news and identified by their fingerprints or teeth marks. She hadn't worked this hard to wind up like that. Hopefully, Xavier was watching his monitors and was trying to get her some help. This was either going to turn out to be a rescue of a lifetime or the end of her life.

Butch pulled Brandon out of the car and toward the warehouse to where Roscoe waited.

"What is going on Roscoe? I can get your money, but I was in the middle of something."

"Yep, you were in the middle of something huh, you and your dick were trying to get in the middle of something alright. I did my time and rotted in that jail for 7 years. You gonna pay me."

"I will pay you, but let this young woman go,"

"I ain't letting her go nowhere. She's next after you,"

"Wait," Brandon took a quick step back, "I'll get your money on Monday, I promise,"

"Monday? You must be out of your damn mind to think I am waiting on Monday for shit. I said today, and I meant today. Monday!? Hell, you could be around the world by Monday! You ain't got my money in that car?"

"No, I was headed there when these guys got in my car and made me drive here,"

"Get him,"

"Wait!"

Mouse hit Brandon in the mouth and blood spewed out everywhere.

"You can't take a punch man. Look at all of that blood. Mouse is just getting started," Roscoe chuckled.

"Shit! Roscoe, you can't get your money if I'm dead," Brandon said as he spits more blood on the ground.

"True, but you are going to be sore when you go get my money you can bet on that," Roscoe insisted.

Annette watched as Roscoe stomped Brandon's leg and Mouse punched him repeatedly. It was gruesome to watch, but Annette knew her job was to continue to signal for help before they started in on her. Butch held on to Annette's arm even tighter, and she knew that she would have a bruise there if she survived. She quickly looked for an escape route, but the room was only lit with two small bulbs overhead. There was seemingly one way in and one way out. She silently prayed for help to come soon.

"Freeze! Stop Police!" A voice in the darkness shouted.

"Shit! I ain't going back," were Roscoe's last words as he took off running.

Annette breathed a sigh of relief.

"Get down miss!" a voice shouted next.

Annette ducked to the ground which made Butch let her go. Once three shots were fired, the noise ceased. Butch put up his hands up and so did Mouse. Roscoe was stopped forever by those three gunshots. Moments later sirens were heard getting louder as they approached the warehouse.

The police called the ambulance, and Brandon Miller was placed on a stretcher alive but beaten severely.

"Annette are you okay?" Xavier, her assistant, went straight to her. He grabbed her and hugged her tightly making sure that she was real. Annette breathed in Xavier strong male scent, but it wasn't Duane so she was very disappointed.

"I'm fine. Where is Duane?" Annette asked.

"I don't know. I spoke to him earlier, but Officer Peaches told him to stay put."

"Oh," Annette said quietly.

"I'm glad that you are all right,"

"Me too. I don't have my phone, purse or briefcase. Can you call the Ruth Chris parking lot to see if somebody found anything?"

"I already have. They have locked it up in their safe. I will get it tomorrow. Right now we need to get out of here,"

"Ms. Jackson, we need to get some information from you before you can leave," an officer said.

"That's fine,"

The officer quickly asked questions which Annette answered to the best of her ability. Xavier chimed in the information that he had been working with the police department and a copy of the recording of what had been videotaped from her jewelry devices would be happily supplied to them if it wasn't on their server already.

Duane arrives at the scene later as Xavier was walking Annette outside of the warehouse.

"Oh my god! Annette are you okay?"

"Yes, I'm okay."

"I have been worried sick. I didn't hear from you, and then I finally looked down and realized that the computer was disconnected. I plugged it back in and saw everything. Did they hurt you?"

"No, I'm alright,"

"I'm so glad," Duane hugged Annette, but he realized that she was not hugging him back.

"Are you ready to go home?"

"Yes I am, and Xavier's going to take me."

"To my place? Why would Xavier need to drive you? I'm here."

"I'm not going to your place. I'm going to my place."

"Why?"

"I'm exhausted, and maybe we can talk in a couple of days."

"A couple of days! I have been out of my mind worrying about you,"

"Really? Why did Xavier get here before you?"

"They told me to stay home, and I did."

"Okay. I believe you. Xavier take me home,"

"Xavier take your hands off of her!"

"Listen Duane! You need to give Annette some space. She said a couple of days, and I think you need to walk away and give her a call in a couple of days,"

"You are not telling me shit about Annette. Annette is my woman, and I am going to take care of her,"

"Really Duane? I didn't see much of that in the past two days. I almost died, and you wouldn't answer your damn phone. I don't have a phone, wallet or nothing! I have to start all over! Get me out of here Xavier,"

"Ms. Jackson, are you okay? Is this gentleman harassing you?" the officer asked.

"No, it's okay, he's just upset. I'm fine. I need to go home and try to recover from this ordeal,"

"Sir, you need to leave this young lady alone. She has been through a lot in the past few hours. Give her 2-3 days to rest and somehow recuperate. If you really care about her, you will give her some time,"

"Annette! Annette! Come on girl! Don't do this! You know me! You know me!" Duane yelled while Xavier put Annette in his car and drove off. Xavier looked at Duane with a mean glare to let him know just how he felt about him at that moment. Duane was gently being held back by the police from approaching the car, but it didn't stop him from yelling even louder.

When the car finally drove off, Duane was released. "Let go of me man!" Duane got in his truck and hit the steering wheel repeatedly as tears of frustration and anger rolled down his face.

Duane dialed his only lifeline at this point, Hank.

"What happened D? Everything alright?"

"He's got her man!"

"Who's got who? Roscoe's got Annette?"

"No, Xavier,"

"Xavier, her assistant?"

"Yes, I was too late, and Xavier took her home,"

"To your house,"

"No! To her house. She didn't want to come home with me. I've lost her. She doesn't know how I feel, and I've lost her,"

"Calm down! What happened?"

Duane tried to explain to Hank everything that happened, but he was too overcome with emotion.

"D, she was scared, kidnapped and exhausted! What else did you think she was going to do?"

"Give her some time," Jasmine chimed in. "She is a loner by nature. She has no family at all. She really has no one in her life that understands her. She needs some down time to get her head together that's all. She loves you,"

"Yeah, D. Listen to Jasmine. Girls talk. Trust what Jasmine is saying,"

"I know what you are saying is right, but she should have gotten in the car with me and gone to my house. We should be picking up some food, heading to the shower together and spend the rest of the night in bed making love and then falling into a coma asleep until morning. That's what should be happening. Instead, I don't know whether she will ever see me again,"

"She will see you again, but in her own time. If you love her, you are going to have to fight for her. Right now, go get you some food, go home, take that shower and go to bed and sleep until in the morning. Try to call her on Monday,"

"Monday! Hell no, I'm not waiting on no Monday!"

"That's what I'm talking about. Get your woman! I'm headed back to bed with mine. Bye!" Hank said.

"Thanks, man," Duane smiled in spite of everything.

"Anytime,"

"I guess we solved Duane's problem again, didn't we?"

"Yeah babe, I guess we did,"

"Well, I've got a problem for you to solve,"

"What's that?"

"I'm hot for you right now,"

"That's not a problem. That's a request,"

"Then, I'm requesting,"

"Say no more,"

Xavier pulls into Annette's driveway with the intent of staying with her the rest of the night. Any woman would be thrilled to have a handsome Latin man take such great care of her, but not Annette. She was thankful for Xavier's hospitality and care, but he wasn't Duane. She had a lot going on in her head about her next steps, and Xavier could tell by the look on her face.

"You okay?" Xavier asked.

"Yes, I am better now after that shower and wonderful meal,"

"If you were mine, I would be busting down that door right now,"

"Yeah, but I'm not yours. We just work together. You know how I feel about Duane. I just need some space for a few days,"

"If you ever change your mind?"

"I know, I will give you a call. Xavier, you are great guy and you know,"

"Please stop right there. I can't take it. I know how you feel about Duane. I just want you to know that I still feel the same way about you,"

"I'm flattered, but we work together and I can't,"

"I get it. I'm going to sleep here on this couch. If you need anything, just yell,"

"I will. Thanks and goodnight,"

"Goodnight," Xavier said quietly. He had told Annette over and over how he felt about her, but this was not the place or the time.

Annette pulled back the sheets of her bed and collapsed under the covers. She thought sleep would come easily, but it didn't. She tossed and turned for hours. She hadn't slept in her own bed for months. She had been at Duane's house, and the smells, surroundings and layout of her bedroom were totally different than his. Besides the logistics, she kept dreaming over and over that she was in that warehouse. She didn't want to yell out and awaken Xavier, so she put a pillow over her face. It was awful. Her body finally took over her mind around 4:00 a.m.

Xavier walked outside onto Annette's porch to smoke a cigarette. His phone rang, "Yeah,"

"You know this shit ain't over,"

"I know but, "

"But nothing. You know what you have to do. We have people waiting,"

"They'll have to wait a little longer,"

"Don't let that bitch and your dick get in between your money and this deal. We've worked too hard, and I've waited long enough. Either you get it, or we will get it and you,"

"Don't you think I know that already? I can't seem to have nothing!"

"Well do what you are supposed to do, and you will have something! Some big money bastard!"

"But..." the phone went silent, and Xavier knew that he couldn't win so he must do what he was told to do. What he wanted more than anything was to run off and build a life with Annette, but he could see it in her eyes that she still loved Duane. No matter how long they had talked about everything before she went to sleep, the love was in her eyes. He remembered his grandmother saying that 'the eyes are the window to the soul.' Annette's eyes were wide open, and all he could see was Duane standing there in those eyes.

Chapter 7

At 7:00 a.m., Annette woke up. She didn't need an alarm. Her body was on automatic pilot. She could have been killed yesterday. There was no family or friends to notify, just Duane, Hank, Jasmine and Xavier. These people were the closest family she had. She was grateful to still be alive. No matter how traumatizing yesterday's events had been, today was a new day. Frightened just a little, to say the least, about what today's events could bring. What would today bring?

Xavier wasn't asleep. He had been sitting up on the couch ever since the phone call. He heard the toilet flush and realized that Annette was awake. He knocked on the door, "You okay in there?"

"Yes, I'm fine, really,"

"You headed back to bed, or are you up for a minute?"

Annette put on a sweats jacket and opened the door of her bedroom, "I'm up. Sleep isn't my friend right now,"

"I get it. You've been through a lot,"

"You got that right,"

"Not to mention. Duane,"

"Duane," Annette said with a long breathy sigh.

"What is going to happen with that?"

"I don't know,"

"Take your time and think about it slowly okay?"

"I will,"

"What are we going to do next about the business?"

"I haven't thought about that either, but I do know that what I've invented is worth far more than I thought,"

"Why do you say that?"

"I believe I was kidnapped, because of what I have created,"

"You think so?"

"Yes,"

"Well, I thought it was a drug dealer and a rich horseman whose business went wrong, and you were caught in the middle of it."

"You think that's all it is?"

"I'm almost positive. Sit down and turn on the TV. I'm going to run out and get some coffee. What kind of coffee do you want?"

"It doesn't matter, just coffee and thank you,"

Xavier opened the door, and Duane was standing there.

"What are you doing here Duane?"

"I am here to see Annette,"

"I thought I said two or three days,"

"I don't give a shit about what you think or said, Xavier. I came to see Annette,"

"It's okay Xavier," Annette walked toward the door in the sweat suit that Duane immediately recognized, because he was there when she bought it.

"You sure? I can stay,"

"You can go," Duane interrupted harshly.

"Duane stop it! Go into the house and wait for me,"

"Thanks for everything Xavier,"

"You are welcome. Call if you need me or tap your bracelet," Xavier said quietly and smiled. He stood in the grass, arms folded and waited until Annette closed the front door before he would get in his car and go to his house.

"That was unnecessary, and you owe him an apology," Annette closed the door behind her.

"I'm sorry, but he's in love with you,"

"I know that, and I've told him that I don't feel the same way about him. He is a friend and co-worker. A damn good co-worker who had my back for real in this situation,"

"I've always had your back!"

"Really Duane, where were you?"

"I know, I know. Let me explain,"

"Explain what? How I called and called you, and you didn't answer? How I have pushed this damn bracelet on my arm until I have a bruised left finger, and you arrived on the scene after Xavier. Did you notice the computer? It should have been videotaping the whole time. What happened?"

"I don't know what happened, but when I got back to the house, I looked down and realized that it was unplugged,"

"Unplugged! What the hell? Unplugged? I have told you not to turn that computer off because it was for security reasons. My security and safety? Why was it turned off?

"I don't know either, but I don't remember bumping into it or actually turning it off! I had so much other stuff going on myself I might have mistakenly turned it off the computer. I didn't do it on purpose. Believe me, please!

"That computer is the transmitter to signal an emergency with my tracking jewelry products and devices. I told you about it long ago! Never unplug this!"

"When my truck blew up, the police came, fire trucks and then Hank came to drive me to get a rental truck."

"Blew up your truck!? Fire trucks, police? When was that?"

"Right after you left the house yesterday morning,"

"You didn't tell me that either,"

"No, I didn't want to scare you or get you involved. I had no idea that Roscoe would have any access to you. I swear on my mother's grave that I would have done differently. You don't understand. They blew up my truck in front of the house! If I hadn't gone to get coffee earlier and left it outside, it would have blown up the whole damn house with you and me in it. I think that's what he was counting on,"

"But, somehow with a twist of fate, I was involved anyway,"

"Yes, God has jokes,"

"No, he is trying to tell your ass something,"

"What?"

"That I really love your ass for real and have your back even if it doesn't feel like you have mine."

"I do have your back. I promise,"

"But right now, I don't feel like you do. When I was telling you all of that stuff about the computer and meeting Miller, you ignored me and didn't take it seriously. You were distant and standoffish as usual. Do you realize that two men have told me how hot I am and one told me he loved me, but you haven't? Not once have you spoken the words! Stupid me, thought you were seeing someone else."

"Never! I only want to be with you. I promise. I have always been a one woman at a time kind of guy. I just don't do juggling relationships at all. I don't want to get hurt, and I sure as hell don't want to purposely hurt someone else. I really..."

"See just then you hesitated and wanted to say something else, but resisted. What is it? Why can't you say that you love me? What is so hard about saying the words?"

"I don't know."

"Yes you do, but you won't tell me. Love is hard, risky and scary. Love is about trust, commitment and all in. I want that. I need that. I deserve that. I work in a man's world. I need a shoulder to lean on after I attempt to slay dragons out here every day. I can't rely on someone who won't say three little words to me and mean it from his heart. I need to hear the words. I can't read your mind. I can't just assume. Assuming is dangerous. More dangerous than even real love. Assuming makes an ass out of me, and I struggled too long and too hard to be made a fool out of. I would rather be alone than pretend. Go! Get out of my place and when you are ready, come back!" Annette yelled through tears.

"No, listen, I called Hank and then called Peaches. While we were talking to Peaches, Xavier called me,"

"Okay, so Xavier basically warned you about what was going on? I get it, get out!" Annette screamed again.

"No, I'm not going nowhere. I do love you! I love you so much it hurts,"

"So now you say the words. I suspect that you realized that you love me when you were about to lose me or worse than that I was about to be killed. They said after they beat up Brandon that I was next. I was scared out of my mind,"

"I'm so sorry about everything. I'm saying the words now,"

"It's a little late,"

"I just hope, I'm not too late,"

"I don't know, I don't know,"

"You know I have loved you all of the time. I just couldn't say the words. Isn't it better to show you and not just tell you? Some dudes are great at saying the words and not faithful or don't know how to show it? I at least show it,"

"I give you that, but why Duane couldn't you say the words. Why?"

This was Duane's chance. He had to tell Annette everything. He had to come correct and tell her or lose her. It was now or never. That little 8-year old's voice would have to be silenced forever. He had relied on it so long and at times, it had brought him closer to the one thing that he missed so much. But, the voice of Hank, Jasmine and Mama Lori were now speaking louder in his head. 'Tell her,' they all said. 'Tell her how you feel, and why you haven't been able to tell her before,' the voices continued to speak louder and louder until he heard his own voice.

"Sit down and calm down. I am going to tell you everything, and you are going to listen," Duane heard himself say.

Annette looked at him and sat down on her love seat and waited. She had cried so much that the tears were dried on her face.

Duane began to pace back and forth in front of that love seat as he did when he was trying to gather his thoughts. He stopped, turned and sat down on the adjacent chair and began.

"Up until I was 5 years old, my life was great. My parents were together in the same house even though they weren't married. My grandparents on both sides weren't married either, so I guess I was surrounded by people that just lived together and not married. They were committed, but not married. I played outside in the street with the other kids, and Hank was my best friend. He lived down the street. Hank was the only white kid in the neighborhood, but he was ours and we all loved him. My dad was killed in a robbery gone badly at the liquor store. My mom was never the same after that. She started hanging out, drinking and partying at the local bar in the neighborhood. I hung out with Hank at his house most of the time. Mama Lori turned into my second mama too. Hank's dad died about a year later after that. My mom's house was paid for, so this guy and his son moved in with us. They were awful both named Roscoe, Roscoe, Sr. and Roscoe, Jr. Roscoe, Jr. was mean to me and was only 3 years older. At 9 years old, he was bad and mean. His dad; Roscoe, Sr. drank, smoked, sold drugs, had started a gang, grooming his son to take over and never worked a regular job. At 7 years old, he started fighting and beating my mom almost every night. It was awful. I would go hide in my closet to try to stop the noise.

One night when I was 8, she finally told him that she couldn't take it anymore and wanted him and his son to get out. He said after living with us these many years, he wasn't leaving and he would kill her before he left. I opened the door of the closet and ran into their room and yelled, 'Mama I love you and let's go anywhere! I don't care about this house. Let's leave now!' I got the worst butt whooping I ever got from that man that night. I still have the scars from that belt. That was the last butt whooping I got from him too. The next day, she packed me a bag and told me to go stay with Mama Lori and Hank. I told her no and that I should stay with her, but she insisted, and I left. That was the last time I saw my mama alive. He killed her that same night by shooting her twice. I think she knew that she was going to die, and didn't want me in the house to witness it. Her sisters cleaned up the house before I was allowed to come back in to get the rest of my things before moving in with Mama Lori. She took me in too. My aunts all kind of wanted me, but mama left a note in her bible that if anything happened to her, let me live with Mama Lori. So I did. I promised myself that I would not tell another living soul else that I loved them. I would show them, but never again say the words. My heart was completely demolished after that. I couldn't believe that someone could be so mean and still sleep with them every night, eat their food and not say thank you when their clothes were washed, ironed and hung up every day. It was horrible. I knew that I had to be a better man than that. Hank and I were officially brothers after that. We worked together everywhere from our paper route to making home deliveries, at the drug store, to the school system and then to IU Roberts Junction. I couldn't focus on school too well after that. Hank was the only reason I passed any of my classes. Mama Lori insisted that we be in the same class in elementary and as many classes as possible in junior high and high school. I had a stable loving home and that was enough for me. I lived with Mama Lori for 10 years. She loved Hank and me like we were her own," Duane stared out into a blank space.

"So how did Roscoe, Jr. come to hate you so much to want you dead?

"It was in high school. I was still living with Mama Lori and Hank. I always wanted to get revenge but didn't know how. I broke into his locker at school and found a bag of money. I stole it. I just had to get even somehow. I took it to the house and showed Hank. It was at least $50,000 in that bag.

I couldn't believe it. I hid it, but what I didn't know is that Roscoe was paying the janitor to keep his secret and the janitor saw me. He told Roscoe about it, and then he came after me. They broke my arm and leg. He would have killed me but because of the code, he didn't."

"What is the code?"

"The code of Roscoe's daddy was that if you already killed a family member, you can only harm or injure another family. The gang was all about family and revenge was limited,"

"That's sounds crazy to me,"

"Me too but it saved my life because they had already killed my mother,"

"What happened to the money?"

"Mama Lori taught me and Hank how to save and invest. I watched Mama Lori when Hank wasn't watching. She called these people that I now know were investment bankers and would tell them how much money to invest. When I turned 21, I called those same people that she did and started investing. She used to say, "You don't have to show your money just be grown and know your money." She taught us to work hard, save a lot and then be able to take care of yourself and your family. She would say, "I didn't have no babies of my own, but I'm going to make sure that you boys know how to work hard, grow your money and know how much money you have at all times." She said, "People who are buying expensive stuff are trying to show off to their friends and family, but the best use of your money is to have it when something happens." I love her for that today."

"Wow, so all of this time you've been playing cheap," Annette smiled for the first time.

"There's that smile I've been missing,"

"Don't change the subject,"

"I'm not, I'm being serious. Yes, I was playing cheap. I have always known that I loved you. But you are so smart, beautiful and gifted, that I know to be with you forever I have to step up my game. I have money, but school is just not my thing,"

"I've never asked you to have a degree have I?"

"No, but I think I should have something. I have 3 years under my belt,"

"Well, you do work at a college campus. What's stopping you?"

"Me."

"So, what are you going to do about it?"

"Finish,"

"That's great Duane. I'm happy for you,"

"Thank you. This has taught me that there is no time like the present. Fate, God, Karma or whatever is out there is not letting me wait,"

"For the record, it is God. I agree you have to go for it. I have been focused on myself, my career and reaching my own goals because I have no one else,"

"You have me if you want me,"

"I'm still upset with you, but I still want you,"

"Well, let me make it up to you,"

"How?"

"First, I have something for you,"

"What?"

"Hold on. I'll be right back," Duane went out to his truck and retrieved something that he knew would move Annette in the right direction.

"Oh my goodness, you found it!"

"Yes, I went to Ruth Chris last night when you wouldn't go home with me and retrieved your purse and briefcase. They almost didn't give it to me, but I convinced them that they should,"

"How did you do that?"

"I showed them all of the pictures of you in my phone and it matched your license,"

"I didn't know you were taking that many pictures of me,"

"Of course; secretly and quietly, but that is the old me. You are going to get tired of me talking so much,"

"I don't think so,"

"We will see,"

"I didn't know if I would ever get this back. Those are my only printed set of plans. In the wrong hands, it could be fatal.

"Well, it's not. Here, they are back, safe and sound,"

"Thank you, Duane!" Annette hugged Duane for the first time since he came to her house. It started out as a friendly thank you hug, but Duane pulled her into his body closer and it turned into something more.

"Oh God, I have missed you,"

"Me, too," Duane pulled back from the embrace and kissed Annette like a starved man on an island. He pulled her into him closer still and swung his legs back so that they landed lying face to face on her couch. Annette was on top of Duane just like they both loved it. Their hands were reaching under clothing for the skin to skin contact when suddenly an alarm went off in Duane's pocket.

"What is that?"

"A reminder,"

"A reminder of what?"

"I've got to make some calls and prepare to surprise you in ways you have never seen before,"

"Right now! Can it wait for two hours or so?"

"Nope, right now! If I don't do this stuff right now, I'll be in bed with you all day and none of my plans will get done. You deserve it. You'll see,"

"Ugh!"

"It will be worth it. You'll see. First, pack a bag with comfortable clothes for 2-3 days. Second, I will be picking you up in 2 hours to take you somewhere, so just wear comfortable clothes, sweats, etc. Don't ask any questions just do like I say. I don't care if that Miller man is in the hospital, I don't trust you to drive anywhere by yourself. It is 8:30 now and I will be back at 10:30. Lock this door behind me when I leave and go pack!"

"Okay,"

Duane stood and wrapped Annette in his arms one more time and kissed her to let her know there would be more to come. They walked to the door and Duane turned and said, "I love you more than you will ever know; but from now on, it will be 'show and tell.' I am going to tell you as much as I show you," he kissed her one more, quick kiss and closed the door behind him.

"We shall see," Annette said quietly and ran to her room to find her luggage. Somehow her phone was fully charged and it rang 20 minutes later.

"Hello,"

"Is this Annette Wilson?"

"Yes, it is,"

"This is Jenny from the Louisville Love the Skin You Are In Spa, and you have an appointment today at 11:00 a.m.," the voice on the line said and gave her additional instructions about the service.

"Thank you, but I didn't schedule an appointment for a spa day."

"No, Mr. Duane Jackson did. See you at 11."

"See you then and thank you,"

When the phone disconnected, Annette thought, 'I guess he is serious about showing as well as telling his love. I wonder what a Brazilian wax is?' She quickly Googled it. 'No!' was her next thought.

Duane knocked on the front door of condo 575 and when the door opened, there stood Xavier. "What do you want?"

"I think we need to talk,"

"About what?"

"About Annette. Can I come in?"

"No, I'll come out there. Let's go for a walk,"

"Alright," Duane said as he followed Xavier a few yards to a small park in his complex.

After sitting down, "Okay Duane, what do you want?"

"I want you to understand how much I love Annette. I realize the mistakes I made and going to give it my fullest attention to right the wrongs,"

"So what does that have to do with me?"

"I need for you to back off of telling Annette how much you love her. If you can keep your feelings separate from your work, I'm cool. Please remain on her team; but as a man and her man, don't come after her. I am asking you. If you don't stop, I am warning you. If you still don't stop, I will stop you. Do I make myself clear?"

"Very clear. But know this; that if you slip up just the slightest, little bit, I will slide right in and take your woman from you. Understood?"

"Understood," Duane extended his hand and Xavier hesitated only slightly, but finally shook his hand. Xavier watched as Duane walked away. He would back off from Annette for now because she had told him how she felt about Duane by the look her eyes. In his mind, he would keep an eye on her just in case Duane slipped up one more time. He realized that he had more important things to tend to at the present.

Chapter 8

Duane had more calls to make to get everything set up for his next steps. His future looked bright and his life was looking happier now more than ever. Annette knew the truth, and he would use every ounce of money and power to prove his love for Annette. He arrived at Annette's place right at 10:30. When she opened the door, he couldn't help but smile. "Hello, beautiful,"

"Thank you, but you just saw me 2 hours ago,"

"I don't care if it was 2 minutes ago. You still are beautiful,"

"Wow, you are about to make me blush. You are making up for a lot,"

"I told you I was, and I meant it. You ready?"

"Yes,"

"Great,"

"So this is the new truck?"

"Yes and no. This is the truck I am renting for now. I should get my new truck when the insurance finalizes everything early next week," Duane said as he opened the passenger door for Annette to sit down.

"Since I haven't been to your place. Did it damage anything else besides the truck?"

"A couple of the garage windows and two of the front windows were shattered but that's all,"

"That's terrible. He wanted you dead didn't he?"

"Yep, but he's dead instead. Thank God,"

Duane reached over the console and took Annette by the hand. "Okay, you're scaring me just a little. What's this all about?" Annette asked.

"I said it was going to be about me showing you as well as telling you,"

"You've never held my hand before,"

"Yes, but I never had anyone blow up my truck, kidnap my girlfriend and almost kill her before either. Life is too damn short,"

"Amen to that. You can hold my hand anytime,"

"Oh, I plan on doing more than this very shortly,"

"Promise?"

"Take it to the bank,"

"I'm counting on it,"

"It's a fact. It's all about you right now, so get used to it,"

"Ummm.." Annette sat back in the seat, smiled and nearly cried. She held tight to Duane's hand. She realized that they were making a fresh start. It was like starting from the beginning. This was a different Duane. Even with the disappointment, it didn't feel this good on their very first date.

"I got your umm. There is more to come," Duane said assuredly. He had worked quickly in those two hours since he last saw Annette and wanted everything to work out perfectly.

They arrived at the "Love the Skin that You are In Spa" and was greeted by a friendly receptionist and Strawberry Mimosas.

"Sir, she should be ready by 3:00 p.m.," the receptionist said.

"Okay. I'll be back then," Duane pulled Annette close for another kiss that nearly spilled her drink. She wasn't prepared for it because Duane was not normally affectionate in public. She realized that with these new changes, she should anticipate anything. Annette was treated like royalty at the spa. They rubbed ever muscle in her body, beat out the kinks in her shoulders from sitting at a computer all day, haircut, style and color, her hands, feet, eyebrows, eyelashes and the Brazilian wax took the visit over the top. She felt like a newborn baby with all her body hair removed. When Duane arrived, he had a fresh haircut, a new outfit on or at least, Annette had not seen the outfit before and a new pair of sneakers.

"Hello gorgeous," Duane said as soon as he saw her. He had pre-paid for the visit and was told that there was nothing to add to his credit card.

"Hello, sir. You look quite handsome yourself,"

"Thank you kindly ma'am! Let's get out of here. You hungry?"

"Starving,"

"Let's get your bag and then out of town first before we eat,"

"Okay, I need a quick shower first and where are we going?"

"Don't worry about it, it is a surprise,"

"Right now I don't know if I like surprises, but I don't have to answer to anyone so it shouldn't matter,"

"Right, so sit back, relax and enjoy the ride. You will enjoy the surprise,"

Duane drove to Annette's place to get her bag when she headed to the shower, Duane said, "I have a request,"

"What is that?"

"Wear a dress with no panties,"

"Oh my, Mr. Jackson, you are about to get nasty, and I think I like it,"

"Girl, I'm going to have you screaming,"

Annette giggled all of the way to the bathroom and was smiling as she came out of her bedroom with a hot little red dress. It was a halter, so she didn't have on a bra either.

Duane put two fingers between his lips and whistled at the outfit, "Girl you look so good, I'm about to change my mind and stay here,"

"No, you are not. We are getting out of here. I need a change of scenery."

"You got it,"

Duane waited on the porch while she secured her office and locked up her house. Given all of the things that had happened in 48 hours, Annette was well aware of her surroundings. Even though she had been on highway I-71 North a million times, she was looking at everything in a whole new way.

"So I have to ask. How did you like the Brazilian thing?"

"I feel like a newborn baby. There is nothing on my, as Oprah says, 'my Va JJ.' Man!"

"Va JJ, what is that? You mean my pussy?"

"No, I mean my pussy."

"It's gonna be mine in just a couple of hours,"

"Whew, that just did something to me. That Brazilian wax thing must get you horny quicker or something,"

"It might have gotten it started, but I'll do the rest,"

"Duane Jackson, what has gotten into you?"

"You and only you. I love you, and I don't care who knows it,"

"Pull over and stop this car,"

"Right now?"

"Right now."

The car was approaching the Shelbyville, KY rest area, and Duane pulled into the truck area and not the car area to park. Annette came across that console and straddled Duane as she kissed him like she hadn't seen him for 10 years. He ripped off her underwear when she lifted up her dress, and her top came down with just one snap. He unzipped his shorts in a flash, and she rode him like a horse at the Derby. When they both climaxed, she continued to sit on top of him and held him inside her. She kissed his mouth and face until he was erect a second time, and took him one more lap around the track. The tall trucks blocked people from seeing their lovemaking; and if it hadn't, it wouldn't have mattered to Duane or Annette who saw them. They had been given another chance at love, and they intended to take it with both hands.

"Dang girl what was that! If I had known I would get that kind of reaction from saying, I love you, I would have done that long ago,"

"Stop teasing me and shut up and drive before I make you pull over again,"

"Don't dare me," Duane said as Annette's stomach growled. "Never mind, your stomach just decided for us,"

They both laughed as Duane pulled back onto the highway.

"You sure you can't tell me where we are going?"

"Nope, trust me,"

"I will,"

"Good,"

In another 30 minutes, they pulled up to the famous Cincinnati Montgomery Inn Boathouse. The restaurant overlooked the Ohio River. The sun was shining and there was a gentle breeze which made the water almost glimmer. Duane was strategic in not taking Annette to a Ruth Chris or any place that would remind her of yesterday's ordeal. His purpose was to have her relax and enjoy their time together. He hoped that he hadn't overwhelmed her too much, but it was all done in love.

"So what's good here?"

"Everything. They are famous for their ribs, but everything is good here,"

"How do you know about this place?"

"Well, Hank and I had to attend a conference here in town one time, and they had a special event here. I always knew that one day I would bring you. Today is the day,"

"Thank you. It's lovely,"

"Welcome,"

The server came to their table and took their drink order. They looked out onto the water for a few minutes, and the server returned with drinks and took their food order.

"Okay, so I have to ask. Are you okay?"

"I haven't had any flashbacks if that is what you are asking. I was so tired from everything that I didn't wake up Friday night, but I'm not so sure about moving forward how I will sleep,"

"Well, hopefully, that spa day and my TLC will help put you into a deep coma-like sleep and not any nightmares," Duane said with a smile

"I hope so too. I'm enjoying the TLC treatment so far," Annette smiled as well and slightly giggled.

"Me too,"

A jazz trio was playing soft music in the background and there was a very small dance floor, so Duane asked her.

"You want to dance?"

"You dance now too?"

"Yeah well, I am going to put these two left feet to good use. I don't care about my two left feet, just wanting to hold you is my only excuse," Duane looked directly into her eyes as he said. He wanted her to know that he meant every word.

"Oh, my. He's suave and sexy now too. Well, remember I have on sandals so don't stomp my brand new pedicure too much,"

"I won't. I don't want those toes to damage my brand new kicks,"

"Oh no! The man has jokes,"

They both laughed as Duane reached out his hand toward Annette, and she easily placed her hand in his. Duane hadn't been much of a hand holder, so Annette was going to take advantage of every opportunity possible to enjoy his touch. Duane brought her into his body close, and Annette fit perfectly under his chin. She rested her head on his chest and breathed in his fresh scent. Duane rested his head gently on the top of hers trying not to mess up her freshly re-combed hairstyle. She didn't seem to mind at all and placed his arms around her waist, and she mirrored his position perfectly. Duane closed his eyes only for a few seconds because he might not see when their hot food would arrive at the table.

"Babe."

"Um?"

"The server is setting our food on the table,"

"Okay, I'm glad you said something because I was about to go to sleep,"

"I could tell. Your breathing was so even. Let's feed you and get you bed early,"

"So what are you trying to say?"

"I'm not trying to say nothing, but let's eat,"

They both laughed with his hand in hers, he leads them back to the table. Annette appreciated all of Duane's efforts to make her feel comfortable and treat her special. She was so hungry that she ate quickly and consumed the massive meal. Duane kept a close eye on Annette to study her reactions to the food, restaurant and her surroundings. He realized that he had taken her for granted. She was God's gift to him, and he should cherish her in every way.

"Why are you staring at me?"

"I almost lost something so precious. I took you for granted. I'm sorry. I am so thankful that I've been given a second chance. I could kick myself. I promise that with everything in me that I won't let you down again,"

"I am glad, but you are still human. You didn't know. You never really know what you have until it's almost gone,"

"Mama Lori used to say, 'you don't miss your water,'

"Until your well runs dry," they said in unison and laughed.

"I know that you are sorry, and I can tell that you are working hard to make it up to me. I appreciate it, but I have a lot in my business to face when I get back home. We also, still have a lot to work on when we get back home,"

"I know. Let's not worry about that now but enjoy our time together," Duane said those words to Annette to ease her mind and his. With his plan well into motion, there would be plenty of time for the recovered work ahead.

The meal ended and a dessert of chocolate cake was devoured with their two spoons colliding at times. Annette yawned for the second time.

"That's the second time that you've yawned. I'm getting the check."

"I'm good," Annette insisted.

"You will be when I get you in bed," Duane leaned in and whispered it into her ear.

"I like the sound of that," she said with a smile.

Duane knew better and signaled for the waiter to bring the check. Annette's adrenaline was wearing off and her body was signaling for rest. Annette grabbed her purse, and Duane reached for her hand as they headed for the door. Duane handed the valet the ticket to retrieve his car. The night air had turned cool, so he put his arm around her to keep her warm until the car arrived. He took Annette by the hand and headed toward the car. When he opened the car door, the driver had not put the car in park and the car jerked suddenly forward.

"Hey man! Put the car in park before she gets in,"

The driver said nothing and didn't open the driver's side car door either. It was dark by now, and Duane couldn't see the driver's face. The light didn't automatically come on inside the car when the door opened, so Duane couldn't see the clothing that the driver was wearing either. The driver jerked the car again, and fortunately, Duane hadn't let go of Annette's hand. Duane pulled Annette back out of the car, and she literally jumped into his arms.

Because of the motion of the car jerking and Duane pulling Annette, the car door slammed and the driver took off.

"Duane!"

"Baby I got you! What the hell! He stole my truck!" Duane yelled. With Annette tight in his arms, "You okay?"

"I think so, but thank God you still had my hand or I would be in that truck with whoever that is. I was half asleep, but I'm wide awake. Do you think someone is trying to kidnap me again? Who did you tell about being here? Who knows? Why? I can't go through that again. Why? What do they want?" Annette was yelling and crying by this time. Twice kidnapped in one weekend would have been too much for either of them to handle especially being out of town unfamiliar surroundings.

"I think they still want those designs you showed at Ruth Chris,"

"I think you are right," Annette opened her purse and quickly began pushing some numbers on her phone.

"Babe, what are you doing?"

"Changing my password on the system. They are too close. Somebody knows too much and seems to be following me everywhere I go or even my next move. I've got to change the sequence on my jewelry too. I don't know who it is, but I can't be too careful,"

"Exactly,"

Just then another valet attendant came running to the entrance area yelling, 'call an ambulance and the police!' While the other valet parking attendant called the police, the yelling attendant ran into the restaurant.

"What the hell? Let's get back to the restaurant quick."

Duane grabbed Annette's hand, and they ran up the six steps back into the restaurant. Fortunately, it was late and only a few tables had occupants. The manager calmly announced that the restaurant would be closing in 15 minutes, and everyone's meal was free.

"Are you two alright?" the manager asked terrified as the police and fire truck sirens were suddenly heard in the distance.

"Physically yeah, but my truck has been stolen with all of our stuff in there and we are not from here,"

"Wait here. Don't leave or catch a cab. We will take care of everything," the manager insisted.

Annette's phone suddenly rang, "Annette are you alright?"

"Xavier? Is that you?"

"Yeah, I saw everything shut down on the system and wondered if something is up?"

Duane shook his head furiously and mouthed, 'don't tell him anything!"

"I'm fine just testing something out on the system that's all,"

"Well, I can't log back in. You going to tell me the password?"

"Not right now we'll discuss it on Monday. I've got to go,"

"Annette! What's going on? You can trust me! I promise!"

"I've got to go right now. I promise we will talk soon,"

"Wait!"

Annette ended the call and realized that there was no one she could trust, but Duane, Hank and Jasmine.

"What did he say?"

"He wanted the password that I just set,"

"I'm not trying to accuse anybody of anything, but why would he need the password? You are the owner of the company, the patents and the inventions. He's just an employee, working for you,"

"I know Duane,"

"Why was he monitoring your system that close anyway?"

"I know, I know,"

"I'm sorry,"

"Me too,"

Dumbfounded, in shock plus tired from everything over the past 2 days, Duane and Annette sat down on the bench just inside the waiting area of the restaurant and watched the commotion outside. They found out that the other attendant was not killed, but passed out unconscious in the parking lot after being hit over the head with a blunt object.

The police arrived to interview Annette and Duane about the events of the entire evening, "I'm Officer John Bowen, and I'm sorry for the circumstances but it is nice to meet you both. Can you describe the person driving your vehicle?"

"My back was to him because I hadn't fully gotten into the truck yet. Duane was helping me in and the driver didn't get out of the truck. I don't know whether his foot slipped or what, but the car jerked and Duane pulled me out of the truck,"

"That's a good thing, ma'am because the assailant could have taken off with you in the truck,"

"He kept looking straight ahead, but I didn't see him because I was looking at Annette and helping her in the truck,"

"I can tell the great love you have for each other, and I'm glad that you were there sir,"

"So am I!" Annette exclaimed

"So am I. Did you know that she was kidnapped on yesterday too? It has been a horrible two days,"

"I am so sorry to hear that. But, I must confess that we have been aware of some activity going on in the tristate area for some time now, but the activity has intensified so that we now can act upon it. Your name and picture were sent through the interstate system when they were trying to locate and track you on yesterday. There is an ongoing investigation of some other activity related to the people involved in your incident yesterday that leads us to believe that you may be in grave danger,"

"Really? Oh my God!"

"What can I do to protect Annette? I couldn't on yesterday, but I be damned if something happens to her today!"

"I totally understand sir. If you give me a few minutes, I will check with my superiors to find out what we can do to help you keep her safe,"

"Oh Duane, this is worse than I thought. I'm in danger and may have gotten you into something as well,"

"It doesn't matter Annette. We are in this together," Duane hugged Annette close and tight to give her the physical reassurance of his words. He was scared to death, but he knew that he had to be strong for Annette. Who knew that the great things that she had invented would now put her in danger?

They waited as Officer John Bowen discussed the situation with his superiors. Duane rocked Annette in his arms like she were a baby. But she was his baby, and he was holding on for dear life.

"Baby, all I can think about is what would have happened if I hadn't been holding on to your hand,"

"Don't say it. I can't bear to think about it myself. My only thought is when is this going to be over?"

"I don't know, but I pray soon if I have anything to do with it. You know I love you more now than ever,"

"I hope so because I am going to need all of your love, the police and God to get me out of this," Annette closed her eyes as she said the words to somehow convince herself that she was going to survive this crazy situation that was not a dream but a horrible nightmare.

In a small bar across town, the phone rang. "Do you have the girl?"

"No,"

"No! What the hell? I told you exactly where she was. All you had to do was pick her up and bring her here!"

"Her dude held on to her, and I took off,"

"You took off in a stolen truck with no girl. What are we going to do with a stolen truck and no girl? She's the brain we need to get the products. He's going to kill us."

"I parked the truck a few blocks away and ran back. The cops, ambulance and fire trucks were everywhere,"

"The cops got them now. We won't ever get 'em."

"Don't say never. They still got to come back home."

"That will be too late, and we won't get the money from the man or the product from the girl,"

"We're dead." The line went dead as well.

"Mr. Jackson and Ms. Wilson," Officer Bowen broke the silence and was not alone and was accompanied by an attractive young female officer stood by his side.

"Yes," Duane and Annette answered in unison as they stood to hear what Officer Bowen would say.

"This is Officer Norma Davis who is my partner on this case. I have talked with my superiors and it was agreed and approved that due to the nature of this case, you both should be taken to one of our safe houses and not to a hotel. If the assailants found you here and confiscated your truck at Montgomery Inn, they will find you at a local hotel. Unbeknownst to many, there are safe houses throughout the area. One is local and called the Forest. The Forest is a heavily secured building built by Rudolph Technologies and utilized by the Police Department as well as other entities who need celebrities and political figures to be safe. There is everything that you need at the Forest except personal items and clothing. Officer Davis and I will accompany you to the nearest store so that you can take care of those needs and then escort you the Forest," Officer Bowen said.

"Thank you," was all that Duane and Annette could say in unison. The things racing through both of their heads ranged from 'this must be a movie' to 'what did I create?'

Duane and Annette were placed in the back seat of an unmarked black SUV and were driven by Officer Bowen and Officer Davis to the closest Walmart where clothing for two days, toiletries and other personal items could be purchased. The entire scene was so surreal. It was like being at the end of a movie where the stars of the movie drive off into the night. Duane held onto Annette's hand the entire time they were in the truck. While looking at the window of the truck, Duane remembered that he hadn't been very affectionate toward Annette in public. Changing that one behavior protected Annette and probably saved her life. When they arrived at the Forest, the garage door opened and they drove into the garage and the truck was lifted into the air on a lift. When the lift stopped, they were told to exit the vehicle. Both Officer Bowen and Officer Davis had to place their hands and faces on a scanner to unlock the door to enter. Once the door opened, all four of them walked into a large wide open spaced room that had few doors and no windows. The only door was to the bedroom and bathroom. The kitchen, dining, living room and recreational areas were all open spaces from that door to the bedroom and bathroom doors. There were wood floors and the furnishings were decorated with fall colors of taupe, green and orange. The Forest was labeled on everything from the furnishings to the floor mats to the doorways to the towels.

"I trust that these accommodations will meet your needs. I am truly sorry for the inconvenience to your lives and what has happened to you both. It is apparent that you both are special young people and someone wants to hurt you, but we are doing everything in our power to solve this case and return you to your lives. You will be here for the night and tomorrow, and I will return with information on your next steps. I suggest that you don't use your cell phones to call anyone. Use these phones that are located in the kitchen or the bedroom only. They are not traceable. Ms. Wilson since you are in the technology business, I believe that you are the primary target and must be the most careful,"

"Ms. Wilson, I am one of many IT specialists as well as a field operative with the department, and that is the primary reason I was assigned to this case.

Have you locked down your system and changed codes or passwords?"

"Yes, I did that before we left the restaurant. I suspect that someone is trying or wanting to get into my system. I locked down my system and condo as well,"

"Is there anyone on your staff that you have shared these codes with?"

"No one, not even Duane,"

"Great. It will protect Mr. Jackson as well,"

Officer Bowen continued to show Duane how to secure the door as Officer Davis talked with Annette. Once the door was closed, they both fell onto the coach in a state of shock. They looked through each cabinet and closet to find something to wear. The only personal items that they had to their name was Annette's purse, her phone, Duane's wallet, his phone and the 3 bags from the local Walmart. What do you do when you are down to your last? When faced with death and survival, what's next?

"I'll be right back," Duane said as he went to the door to secure it one more time. While returning to the bedroom, he stopped and leaned over the counter to gather his thoughts and courage to face her. He remembered being in a similar situation with Hank when he was in trouble, but this was different. This was the second time in a few days that he and Annette's safety was in jeopardy. He hoped that the billionaire horseman and Roscoe the rat weren't a part of this too. Roscoe was dead, but the billionaire was not. Annette wasn't just anybody, she was and always would be the love of his life. He wasn't safe either, but if anything happened to Annette, he couldn't bear to think of it. What was yelling in his head was that evil voice taunting him that he should have never admitted to Annette that he loved her. He couldn't dwell on that now and must silence that voice if he were to get any sleep tonight. His job was to stick by her side and keep her as safe as possible. He pushed himself away from the counter and headed toward the bedroom. The oven light was kept on and there were motion sensor night lights the illuminated as he walked down the hall.

The closer he got to the bedroom, the louder the shower water became. He stood in the doorway and just watched Annette go through her normal routine of lathering her sponge and covering her body. Duane realized that he wanted to be the sponge and cover her body immediately. He removed his clothes and left them lying on the floor at the entrance. When he opened the shower door, she gasped.

"You scared me,"

"I'm sorry. I just wanted to join you, because the sponge was making me jealous,"

"Oh yeah?"

"Yeah," Annette dropped the sponge on the shower floor and handed him the body wash. As Duane's hands were filled with bubbled lather and they gently applied the soap to every inch of her body. He kissed her mouth, and his hands moved from her neck to her arms and cupped her breasts. He massaged them softly until her nipples became round as grapes, and he turned her toward so her back was against the water to remove the soap he replaced it with his mouth. He sucked her breast as to suck the life out of her into himself. He could hear her moan with pleasure; but more importantly, he could feel her moans vibrating through her chest to his mouth. His tongue pleasured each one to make her moan even louder, and his hands hadn't gotten lower than her waist. His hands almost met at the middle of her small waist as he moved from up and down her back and around her mid-section. More soap was applied to his hands before he headed down to his own pleasure spot, her vagina. He intended to just lather her and rinse her off with the removable shower head and let it do its magic, but three of his fingers on his right hand got jealous of the shower head and crept inside.

She screamed, "Duane! I love you so much!" The tears of pain and pleasure flowed down Annette's face.

"Don't cry, baby. I got you. I love you now more than ever. Just enjoy me loving you,"

So what do you do when faced with life and death, you love as hard as you can and don't stop.

Duane dropped to his knees and placed his mouth where his fingers had been. As his nose teased her clitoris, his tongue dipped where his fingers had been and drover her repeatedly to orgasm heaven. Her knees became weak, and he caught her by the buttocks with both hands and placed both her legs over his shoulders and she landed up against the shower wall. His tongue and mouth pleased her until her mid-section landed on his head from the power of the orgasm. He placed her gently on her feet while she stood and said, "It's not over, it's my turn,"

Annette gathered soap in her hands until it became a soapy lather, and she began rubbing his head, neck down to his stomach. "Turn around," was her command as she lathered his back down his buttocks to his feet.

"You know baby,"

"Please don't say anything,"

"Your wish is my command,"

"That's what I like to hear. Turn around again, so I can touch my favorite part,"

She massaged his penis until it was fully erect. She used that same shower head to rinse his body; but once the soap was gone, to her knees she went for her mouth to give the same pleasure to Duane as he had given to her.

"Baby, oh shit,"

"Ssssh," was all that Annette could say. Normally Duane wasn't a talker, but he didn't want things left unsaid. Words were unnecessary, and his body felt so good he couldn't get any understandable words out anyway. Moans and grunts were exiting his mouth, and he held onto the walls to keep standing at her glorious demonstration.

She sucked him dry, massaged his balls for more and he came in her mouth with a bass scream of release.

They showered again quickly and dried each other with the towels which quickly lead to the bedroom and into "Round two," Duane said as he inserted his penis into Annette's pleasure pussy in her favorite position, doggy style while hard and fast.

"Round three, it's my turn," Annette said as she rode Duane slow while on top. She knew how to tighten her vagina walls to make him scream, shout and cuss with pleasure. He and his penis were all hers to do with as she wanted. He didn't care. He just laid back and enjoyed the ride. Afterward, they fell into a love and exhaustion-induced coma and slept soundly.

In the morning, Hank's phone rang on the nightstand.

"Hello,"

"We are in trouble again!"

"Duane?"

"Yeah, it's me,"

"This is not your number or your ringtone,"

"I know. Is Jasmine awake?"

"She wasn't, but she is now,"

"Good, put me on speaker phone,"

"What happened?"

"They tried to kidnap Annette again,"

"Who did?"

"We don't know exactly, but we are now at a safe house in protective custody of the Cincinnati Police Department,"

"What the hell?" Hank and Jasmine exclaimed in unison.

"We agree. Imagine being in our shoes. It was horrible," Duane said as he and Annette began to relay the details of the past 3-6 hours.

"So what's next?"

"We've got to wait on the Cincinnati Police to tell us whether they found the truck and what we can do next. We may need a ride home,"

"I'm there. Tell me where and when,"

"I don't want you and Jasmine to be endangered, but I may need..."

"Stop right there. Jasmine and the babies can stay with her parents,"

"No, if you are going, I am going. The babies can stay with my parents. This lady is going with you, baby,"

"I guess that is settled, you guys need to tell me. Hold on, this is Peaches. Let me see if I can patch her in,"

"What the hell has Duane gotten himself into now?"

"Hold on Peaches," Hank conferenced Peaches in with Duane on the call. "Duane? Peaches?"

"Yeah,"

"I'm here,"

"Go ahead Peaches,"

"What's going on Duane? I know the gist of it because I am looking at it on my computer screen, but you guys fill me in,"

Duane and Annette retold the details to Peaches. She told them that Officers Bowen and Davis in Cincinnati were highly recommended, and they should trust them. She also let them know who was assigned to the Miller and Roscoe case there in Louisville. If they didn't meet those 4 officers, don't trust anyone. This case went high up and even International.

"Interpol is working on some connections overseas to track who is behind this,"

"Interpol? The international police!"

"This sounds like something in a movie,"

"Your movie fool. Annette, those tracking devices are literally worth millions and maybe even billions. Miller wasn't meeting you for nothing. We are working with them so we can track down who is behind all of this. We want to know specifically why Kentucky and why specifically you? What are the next steps today?"

"We were told that they would be back to fill us in on the details at 1:00 p.m. today,"

"It is 10:30 now. So you guys just sit tight. Don't leave there for anything until you hear from them,"

"Got it,"

"I wouldn't use your regular cell phones until this is settled. There is tracking on them as you know Annette. Did you guys buy a trac phone?"

"Yes, it's charged but we haven't activated it yet,"

"Activate it via the safe house phone when we hang up,"

"Let me know when you guys need that ride, and Jasmine and I will come up to get you guys,"

"You are not going anywhere near them Hank! You hear me. My family or them babies of mine can't be at risk at all with these crazies we are working with here. These are not project crack heads and thugs, these are high-level professional criminals and killers,"

"What about my job? How long will I be in custody?"

"We are connecting with IU on Monday for you. You can't reach out to them because of your situation. I am suggesting to my superiors that they either contract Hank to run the department temporarily or is your assistant capable of handling it?"

"I guess so, but this would be the first time seeing what he can do,"

"Well, I'll let you know what is decided on that situation.   Annette, what is your business situation?"

"My servers and information are on lockdown, but my condo has a security system and those plans are in my safe at the condo. That doesn't guarantee that they can't break into my condo and bust open my safe. If they are professionals, we are not really safe?"

"Right now you are, but in the open, you are not safe. I'm sorry, but I must be honest with you. Stay put and wait for Officer Bowen,"

"Will do,"

"Duane, you guys be safe. Hank, you guys stay put. I'm getting too old for this, but we got Hank out of trouble last year and this year, it is Duane and Annette's turn.   The life of a police officer. Retirement can't come soon enough,"

"Thanks, Peaches, I owe you my life literally,"

"Well, a great steak dinner at a nice restaurant might help me feel just a little bit better,"

"When this is over, dinner is on me,"

"On us,"

"Sounds even better. Talk to you guys later,"

Peaches hung up the phone leaving Hank and Jasmine still on the line.

"This situation and you guy's loyalty to each other has gone way past years of friendship. I don't know how I will ever repay you, Hank,"

"You've saved my life a time or two, so just get home safe that's all,"

"That's the plan,"

"I don't care what Peaches says if you need me call me. Take care of you and Annette, D. Love you man,"

"Love you and Jasmine for life Hank,"

"It sounds great when you say it,"

"It sounds good saying it too,"

"Bye,"

"Bye,"

There was an hour before Officer Bowen and Davis were scheduled to arrive at 1:00 p.m. It didn't take Duane and Annette long to shower, eat a quick breakfast and wait. There was nothing really to pack in the newly purchased backpacks so they were sitting and watching the security screen when it buzzed. Officer Bowen was seen on the screen with someone else that clearly didn't look like Officer Davis. Peaches had told them that he could be trusted, so they waited. The buzzer sounded, and Duane hit the talk button, "Good morning,"

"Good morning to you too. I have brought breakfast with me and it's full of Cincinnati Pig," Officer Bowen said as he showed them the bag.

"Let's go!" Duane quickly said to Annette who grabbed her backpack and headed to the escape entrance through the closet door in the bedroom.

"No problem, I'll buzz you right up," Duane said calmly as he followed her.

Pig was the code word if something was clearly wrong when they were to return for Duane and Annette. They had been instructed to go to the escape elevator through the bedroom closet, and there would be a car waiting for them when the door opened. It was only to be used in emergencies and would alert the special police task force. Once in the car, they were to go straight to the police station and make no stops.

When the elevator opened, it was just as Officer Bowen had said, a car waiting.

Annette called Hank while Duane sped to the station. "Hank, something went wrong when the police came to get us. We are headed to the police station, we might need you and Jasmine to come and get us,"

"Don't worry, Peaches changed her mind and came to get us already, and we are on our way. She told us a little bit about what happened, and we want to be there for you guys no matter what. We will meet you at the Police Station, don't stop for anything or anyone until you get there! Love you both!"

Hank and Jasmine were in an unmarked SUV with the newly promoted Special Agent Peaches in the passenger seat along with another Special Agent flown in from Washington. The red and blue lights inside the headlights and the sirens were screaming for drivers to pull over or get out of the way. They were traveling at high rate of speed between 80-90 miles per hour. Hank held Jasmine's hand, and they literally prayed all of the way to Cincinnati for the safety of their family, Duane and Annette. No recently released movie in the theater could compare to what they were currently experiencing.

Meanwhile, Duane and Annette were racing across town in one of the latest model cars. Annette periodically looked back to see if they were being followed. Since being kidnapped only 2 days ago and now running from whoever wanted her dead, she could not be too cautious for her and Duane's sake. Duane had closed the closet door prior to going down on the elevator to give Officer Bowen more time, but he drove as fast as possible as Annette watched. They couldn't tell if they were being pursued or not, but Annette felt like she had to do something, so she kept looking. The car was complete with a push-button start system, and an advanced GPS system complete with a two-way communication so that Duane and Annette could see and hear the officer speaking.

"Mr. Duane Jackson, this is Special Agent Otis Golden."

"Yes?" Annette and Duane yelled simultaneously.

"Take your hands off of the wheel and take your foot off of the gas pedal. I will take it from here." It was like magic. Duane removed his hands and took Annette by the hands as he lifted his right foot off of the accelerator. The car was on auto-pilot and remotely accessed by Agent Golden. He literally drove the car with Duane and Annette just sitting there in awe watching the car move by itself through the streets of Cincinnati until it turned into a normal looking parking garage. The car drove down to the second lower level of the garage and parked into an empty parking space in front of a wall. The car blinked the headlights twice, the wall slowly moved to the right and a stainless-steel door appeared similar to a regular elevator door but much larger. The car horn sounded once, the stainless-steel door parted in the center and the car drove onto the platform. The steel door closed behind the car and slowly the car with Duane and Annette inside descended even lower. Duane held onto Annette even closer and whispered, "I love you no matter what."

"I love you more," Annette said as she kissed him. The unknown makes you grasp tightly what you do know and have.

The lift stopped suddenly while making a swishing sound. The door opened and the car literally drove a few feet and then stopped in front of another door. "Please exit the vehicle," the voice on the GPS system said.

Annette and Duane gathered their few belongings and exited the car. Once the car doors closed, a voice from overhead said, "thank you for your cooperation. Please walk toward the door and as you approach it, the door will open."

The door opened to a fully functional control room. They were met by Special Agent Golden, "I'm Officer Golden who drove the car here. Mr. Jackson and Ms. Wilson. Welcome to the Interpol Ohio Unit."

"Interpol?"

"Yes, Interpol. Somehow, Ms. Wilson, you and what you have invented is wanted by some very unscrupulous people."

"Who?" Annette asked.

Agent Golden opened a folder and several images were laid out on the table. Just then the same door that Annette and Duane came through was opened and in walked, Hank, Jasmine, newly appointed Special Agent Pamela "Peaches" Simpson and two other officers were following them.

"Thank God you are alright," Jasmine said as she hugged Annette as tight as possible.

"I have had the weekend from heaven and hell if you know what I mean,"

"Girl, don't I know it," Jasmine replied.

"D, you're alive man,"

"Yeah, thanks, Hank. I hate you got involved,"

"If it's you, I'm involved. We are brothers for life remember,"

"I remember,"

"Well, since Special Agent Simpson is here. I'll let her take over and bring you up to speed,"

"Thank you, Agent Golden. It seems that Louisville, KY of all places has become a hot spot for human trafficking in addition to drugs. Your invention Annette has caused quite a stir, and they are attempting to get your invention off the market so that it will make it harder for these victims to be found. There is another group that wants to purchase your invention, but for other criminal reasons. They want to use the devices to track and trace drugs, guns and other packages. There is literally a war going on in the underground for your invention,"

"Really? I knew it could have an impact, but nothing like this,"

"Well, our biggest problem is this man right here," Peaches opened an envelope and threw an 8 x 10 photo on the table on top of all of the other pictures on the table for all to see.

"Xavier!" Annette cried.